HIGH SCHOOL MUSICAL

STORIES FROM EAST HIGH
SUPER SPECIAL

UNDER THE STARS

HIGH SCHOOL MUSICAL

STORIES FROM EAST HIGH
SUPER SPECIAL

UNDER THE STARS

By Helen Perelman

Based on the Disney Channel Original Movie
"High School Musical," Written by Peter Barsocchini
Based on "High School Musical 2," Written by Peter Barsocchini
Based on Characters Created by Peter Barsocchini

Disney
PRESS

New York
An Imprint of Disney Book Group

Printed in the United States of America

First Edition
1 3 5 7 9 10 8 6 4 2

Library of Congress Catalog Card Number: 2008920358
ISBN: 978-1-4231-0913-6

For more Disney Press fun, visit www.disneybooks.com
Visit DisneyChannel.com

CHAPTER ONE

Troy Bolton tapped his pencil on his desk to the beat of the song in his head. He had gotten to Mr. Gold's third-period environmental science class early and was watching the students file into the room. He nodded to his basketball-team buddies Chad Danforth and Jason Cross as they strolled in the door.

"Hey, Troy!" Chad called. "What's up?"

"Nothing much," Troy said, flipping his pencil in his hand. "You finish the assignment?"

"Yup," Chad answered. "Jason and I got the job done last night."

Jason reached over and traded high fives with Chad. "And we managed to catch a movie, too."

"Hi, Troy!" Sharpay Evans called as she waltzed into the room. She threw her head back and flashed Troy one of her megawatt smiles. "Did you do the assignment?"

"I did," Troy said. "Gabriella and I worked on it last night. It was a pretty cool experiment."

Sharpay made a face as she sat in the seat in front of him. Ever since Troy met Gabriella Montez, they had been inseparable. And now that they were in the same science class, they were even doing schoolwork together. It was too cute for Sharpay's taste.

"Ryan finished up ours this morning," she said, flipping her blonde hair. "My brother and I aced it, I'm sure. I am *so* getting a new convertible at the end of the semester. My dad said that if I get all As, the car is mine. So far, so good."

"You seem pretty confident. The semester just started," Chad chimed in.

Sharpay shot Chad a look that could have frozen a steamy cup of hot cocoa. "Well, whatever," she said, turning around in her seat.

Troy's eyes went back to the door. Taylor McKessie and Kelsi Nielsen entered the room, happily chatting. Gabriella had class with Taylor and Kelsi second period and they usually walked to environmental science together. It was strange that she wouldn't be with them.

Before Troy could even ask, Taylor called over to him. She could see his worried expression from across the room.

"She's coming!" Taylor reassured him. "Ms. Darbus wanted Gabriella to take something down to the front office for her," she added as she sat down next to him.

Taylor was about to go on, when Chad's voice rang out. "Hey, Taylor," he said, flashing her a sparkling grin. It was no secret that he had a pretty big crush on her.

Taylor looked up at Chad and smiled sweetly. "Hey, there," she said.

The bell for third period rang just as Gabriella rushed into the classroom. She looked over at Troy and waved.

"See," Taylor said, leaning over to Troy. "No worries. Gabriella would never be late for *this* class."

"Okay, everyone," Mr. Gold said. "Take your seats." He was standing at the blackboard, a big grin on his face. "I have some great news!"

Sliding into her seat, Gabriella sat two rows behind Troy. He turned around and gave her a wink. Troy was always a pretty good student in science, but this year, thanks to Gabriella, he had a new appreciation for the sciences. She was not only supersmart about the subject, she also enjoyed sharing her enthusiasm with Troy.

"Good morning," Mr. Gold said, still trying to quiet the class. "As I said, I have some exciting news to share. My two environmental studies classes have been approved for a special

4

field-trip program, Living Things in the Ecological Environment."

"That sounds as exciting as a trip to the doctor's office," mumbled Chad.

"Hold on," Troy whispered. "Let's hear him out."

"We'll be cataloging the flora and fauna at a state-park camping ground," Mr. Gold said. "Including the indigenous aquatic, amphibious, avian, and mammalian species."

"Can you say that again in English?" Jason called out.

Mr. Gold continued. "Quite simply, we'll be sleeping in tents, going on hikes, testing the water for different elements, and looking at the wildlife."

"All right!" Chad exclaimed, jumping up to hit high fives, first with Troy and then Jason. "We're taking a walk on the wild side!"

"So we'll be performing science experiments in the wilderness?" Taylor asked, as she took careful notes.

"Yes," Mr. Gold replied. "It's a chance for science to come alive for all of you. This is a unique experience. We will have a team of rangers to chaperone and teach us. Plus, Ms. Darbus has agreed to come along as well."

The whole time Mr. Gold had been speaking, Sharpay sat with her lip turned up in a snarl. "Sleeping in tents?" she finally said. Her idea of roughing it was when the cleaners ruined her silk sheets and she had to use cotton ones instead. Outdoor sleeping was definitely not her style. Shaking her head, she added, "I don't think so."

But the rest of the class didn't seem to mind. As the big news sunk in, everyone started talking at once.

"Hold on," Mr. Gold said. "Settle down." He raised up his hands to quiet the class. "I know that you all have a lot of questions. I am going to pass out these booklets which will explain all the details." He pointed to a large stack of neatly piled packages on the front table. "Please take the packets home and discuss with your parents. All consent forms are due back at the end of this week. The field trip will take place over the three-day holiday weekend coming up in a couple of weeks. We'll leave on a Friday morning and be back Monday."

"Dude," Chad said, leaning in toward Troy. "I am all about the great outdoors. This is going to be awesome! We'll all be hanging out together. What could be better?"

Mr. Gold stood behind Chad, a packet in his hand. He cleared his throat. "Sorry to disappoint you, Mr. Danforth, but there will be plenty of *work* being done. If you check this packet, you'll see that we'll be very busy. And please note, there will be ample time to earn extra credit, which I know many of you are interested in doing." He slapped the packet down in front of Chad and then moved on, handing out the rest.

"I definitely like the idea of some extra credit," Kelsi whispered to Gabriella. Both girls were already sold on the idea of the trip.

"Now that that is taken care of, please pass in the assignments that you completed with your partners," Mr. Gold announced when he returned to the front of the room. "And then let's get today's lesson started."

"Mr. Gold!" Sharpay called out, raising her hand high in the air. "Ryan has our assignment and he is in the fifth-period class."

Mr. Gold shook his head. "I'm sorry, Sharpay, but as I explained to you earlier, your partner needed to be in *this* class," he said. "And your brother is in the fifth-period class."

"Well, that wasn't very clear to me," Sharpay tried to explain. "Ryan and I do everything together. We're a superstar team."

"That might be true," Mr. Gold replied. "But regardless, Ryan isn't in this class."

Sharpay huffed and puffed, but Mr. Gold continued with the day's lesson.

Despite his best efforts, most of the students in the class weren't really paying attention to Mr. Gold, who was standing next to a chart at the front of the room. They were all sneaking peeks at their packets. When the bell finally rang, the chatter was all about the upcoming trip.

Gabriella gathered her books and then walked over to leave with Troy.

"The trip sounds pretty cool, huh?" he asked as they both made their way out of the classroom. His brain was spinning with the idea of hanging out with Gabriella for a whole weekend.

"I love camping," Gabriella said, hugging her books tightly. "My mom and I used to go all the time when I was little. Have you ever been?"

"Once, when I was a Boy Scout," Troy said with a laugh as they walked through the door. "But my dad got poison ivy, and we had to come home early."

As soon as Sharpay was sure everyone had left the room, she walked over to Mr. Gold.

"Mr. Gold," Sharpay cooed. "Now, I really don't think this trip is something that I can do." She sat down on a desk and looked directly at her teacher. "As you can see, I'm not much of an outdoor girl."

"What do you mean, Sharpay?" Mr. Gold asked, giving her a hard look. "This is a great opportunity for you to learn science hands-on. If you are as serious as you said about doing well in this class, I suggest that you reconsider. This trip could boost your grade. You'll be able to earn some extra-credit points. And since I'm going to have to deduct points from your most recent assignment, as you did not follow the rules, those points could be a big help come the end of the year."

Sharpay weighed the options in her head. "You mean if I go on this trip, I'll get the good grade I deserve?"

"Well," Mr. Gold said, "you'll have to do the work on the trip, not just go." Then he pointed to the packet in Sharpay's hand. "Did you have a chance to glance through the materials yet?"

"No," Sharpay confessed, shaking her head. She looked at the packet.

"You might be interested to learn that there is a special horseback-riding session." Mr. Gold watched Sharpay's eyes light up. "I believe you once told me that you are a championship rider. We could use someone like you out on the trail."

"Horses?" Sharpay squealed. She sat up a bit straighter. "I love horses! And I do happen to be an expert rider."

Smiling, Sharpay pictured herself riding a handsome stallion through the woods. Then she imagined herself driving into the school parking lot in that beautiful new convertible she had seen in the showroom a few weeks ago. If she could get her grade up with a camping trip and a horse ride, maybe she should reconsider.

"Okay," Sharpay said, picking up her books. "I'll think about it."

Mr. Gold smiled. "I hope that you do."

Later, during lunch, Zeke Baylor saw Sharpay on line in the cafeteria. He had, to his own surprise, developed a crush on Sharpay and now took every opportunity to talk to her. Some people thought Sharpay was a bit over-the-top, but Zeke didn't see her that way. To him, she was the sweetest pastry he'd ever seen. He raced over to her as she approached the hot food.

"The ziti doesn't look so bad," Zeke said. "You should try it." Being a baker, Zeke knew all about food and cooking.

"Um, no thanks," Sharpay replied as she viewed the steaming pan of pasta. She pushed her tray past the hot-food entrées to the salad bar.

"So are you going on Mr. Gold's eco weekend?" Zeke asked, trailing behind her. He had been in the other environmental science class and so had no idea what she thought of it.

Sharpay flipped her hair back. "Totally. I wouldn't miss it." After her talk with Mr. Gold, she had decided the weekend—and the extra credit—wouldn't be so bad.

"Really?" Zeke said. In all honesty, he hadn't

12

expected Sharpay to go. Sharpay and camping didn't seem to be a likely combination.

"I once played Annie Oakley and loved the camping-out scenes," Sharpay said as she reached for a plate. "Besides, I really need the extra credit." She piled up some carrots and mushrooms on a heap of lettuce. "I am so close to getting that new car my dad promised me." She scanned the other vegetables and then pushed her tray along. "And there's going to be a trail ride," she added. "I've been riding horses since I was little. I've competed in a ton of shows. I adore horses, don't you?"

"Horseback riding?" Zeke asked. He didn't remember hearing about any horses on this trip—just science experiments.

Sharpay nodded. "Mr. Gold told me about it," she said. "Do you ride?" She picked up a chocolate-chip cookie and continued moving down the line to the cash register.

"Oh, yeah," Zeke said, the lie just flying out of his mouth. The truth was that he had only ridden once in his life—and it had been a total disaster.

A couple of years ago, the Wildcats went for a two-week basketball camp where there happened to be stables. On the first day, the team went on a trail ride. Zeke's horse threw him off, and while he didn't get hurt, he vowed never to get on another horse again. He couldn't even walk past the stables for the rest of the trip without breaking into a sweat.

But as Zeke followed Sharpay to the register, he found himself digging himself into a deeper hole. "Yeah, I love horses. I'm an excellent rider."

As the words left his mouth, Zeke wanted to hit himself in the head. Why didn't he just stay quiet?

"Cool," she replied. "Maybe we can ride together." She gave him a smile and turned to walk toward her table.

"What was that about?" Troy asked, coming up behind Zeke and following his friend's gaze.

"Sharpay just asked me to go horseback riding

with her," Zeke said with a far-off, dreamy look in his eyes.

"You finally won her over, huh?" Troy asked with a grin. He gently slapped his friend on the back as they walked over to join Chad and Jason at a table. "All those treats you baked for her must have made a good impression."

Zeke shook his head as he sat down. He knew Sharpay had a sweet tooth and had enjoyed his baked treats, but that hadn't gotten him very far. Apparently there was a better way to get her attention. Forget the éclairs and soufflés. "The sweets might have helped a little bit," he admitted as he watched Sharpay, who was now across the room eating her lunch. "But it seems the way to her heart involves a horseback ride."

"Dude, you don't ride," Chad said with his mouth full of sandwich.

"Yeah," Jason piped up. "After your fall, you walked the long way to the dining hall every meal for the rest of camp so you wouldn't have to pass the stables."

Troy agreed. "You wouldn't even get on the carousel at the state fair last month!"

Waving his hand in front of his face, Zeke dismissed his friends' comments. "Nah, that was silly. I can ride. It can't be that hard to get back in the saddle."

"You're serious?" Chad asked.

"Totally," Zeke said.

Troy took a bite of his ziti and eyed his friends. "This camping trip is going to be one wild ride!"

CHAPTER TWO

Gabriella reached for the backpack and sleeping bag in the trunk of her mother's car. She balanced both of them on her shoulders and then she walked up and leaned in the driver's-side window.

"Bye, Mom," she said, giving her mother a quick kiss on the cheek.

"Don't forget the bug spray at night," her mother warned. "You know how those mosquitoes come out when the sun goes down." Then her face softened, and she gave her daughter a warm smile. "And don't forget to have a great time, sweetheart."

"Thanks, Mom," Gabriella sang out. Giving her mother one final smile, she toted her stuffed backpack and sleeping bag over to the large bus at the far end of the school parking lot. It was strange being at school so early, before all the faculty cars were lined up in the staff lot. Mr. Gold had said that the buses would leave at seven a.m.—sharp. He wanted to get up to the campsite and start working right away.

"That's all you're bringing?" Sharpay sniped when Gabriella walked over and put her bag on the ground.

"It's not a very long trip," Gabriella said. She eyed the large, bright pink-and-gold trunk at Sharpay's feet. "What's in there?"

"A girl needs to be prepared," Ashley Appleton answered before Sharpay could. She gave Sharpay two quick air kisses. "Am I right? Or am I right?" Like Gabriella, Ashley was new to East High, but unlike Gabriella, she usually didn't have very nice things to say.

"You are *so* right," Sharpay cooed.

Gabriella's gaze moved past the trunk, and she noticed that there were six additional pieces of luggage.

"You've got to be kidding," Gabriella said with a laugh. She gestured to the luggage surrounding Sharpay. "This is *all* yours?"

Looking around her, Sharpay spotted a blue duffel that didn't match her six piece set. "Uh, no," she said, pointing to the small bag. "That's Ryan's."

Gabriella sighed and left Sharpay. She moved toward the bus, where she quickly spotted Kelsi and Taylor.

"Hi, guys!" she called.

"Are you ready for the greatest field trip of all time?" Taylor asked. "I am so excited about the hands-on science. I'll bet that we get to do a lot of cool experiments."

"I'm psyched to be outside," Kelsi added. "I

read that this park is known for its wildlife and since you are so far from any cities, you get amazing views of the night sky. You don't even need a telescope to see constellations."

"Yeah," Taylor agreed. "I heard that on the last night we're going to have a special class where we look at the stars."

"Cool," Gabriella said. Then she thought about how nice it would be to gaze up at the stars with Troy. She smiled. "This is definitely going to be a great trip."

"If we survive the long bus ride," Taylor whined. "I am dreading that."

As if on cue, Chad appeared by Taylor's side and gave her shoulder a squeeze. "Don't worry about that," he said. "I downloaded a great playlist for you to listen to." He winked at Taylor and pulled out two pairs of earphones from his back pocket. "Look, I brought an extra pair for you." He dangled the wires in front of Taylor.

Before Taylor could even respond, Chad announced that he was going to find them seats. With a broad smile, he headed to the bus.

"That was sweet," Kelsi said when Chad was out of earshot. Anyone who took the time to compile their own playlist was okay in her book. Kelsi was very into all things musical, especially *making* music.

"I guess," Taylor said. She herself seemed a little unsure of Chad's musical taste—and the gesture. Nevertheless, she had a smile on her face as she followed him to the bus.

Seeing her friend's smile made Gabriella think of Troy. She scanned the crowd, looking for his shaggy brown hair.

Kelsi noticed Gabriella's gaze. She knew that look in her friend's eye. "Troy's over there," she told her, pointing across the parking lot. She picked up her bag and walked toward the bus. "I'll see you aboard!"

On the far side of the lot, Troy was standing with his dad. Troy's father was also the coach of the boys' varsity basketball team. It seemed there was never a moment without some team matter to discuss. Even though it wasn't basketball season, Gabriella would have guessed that Coach Bolton was giving some advice to his varsity captain.

Before she could go over and find out for sure, Mr. Gold stepped off the bus. "Come on, East High!" he shouted. "Let's get a move on it! We need to be at the campground by lunch."

The rest of the Wildcats moved toward the bus. Ms. Darbus, who was dressed in an electric blue warm-up suit, was greeting and checking in the students as they boarded.

"Let's go, students!" she called cheerfully. "Everyone come on and find a seat."

Struggling with her luggage, Sharpay hadn't moved from the spot where her father had dropped her off. She tried to pull one of the large suitcases, but it kept falling over. Even though some of the suitcases were on wheels, the bulking masses were hard to maneuver. Zeke ran over to Sharpay.

"Let me help you with that," he said, seizing

the opportunity to get closer to Sharpay by handling her luggage.

"Thanks," Sharpay said. She curled up her lip in disgust and then pointed to her brother. "Ryan was no help."

Although he didn't say it, Zeke could see why Ryan wanted nothing to do with these bags. "What did you do?" Zeke asked as he huffed and puffed, struggling to lift and pull each of the bags. "Pack rocks?"

Throwing her head back, Sharpay tossed her hair a few times. "Oh, don't be silly," she scoffed. "You know that I have to be prepared for every costume change."

"Why? Are you performing?" Zeke asked. He wouldn't be surprised if Sharpay had planned a whole musical dance routine for up at the campground. Stage or no stage, she would want to be front and center.

"Well, no," Sharpay confessed. "But then again, you never know."

Mr. Gold had anticipated needing a separate

truck for the gear and luggage, but as he eyed Sharpay's complete set he knew that he had to enforce some rules.

"Sharpay, the packet that I handed out to the class clearly stated one bag per student," Mr. Gold told her as she approached.

Pouting, Sharpay did a mental check of all of the things that she had packed in her bags. "But I need everything here," she declared. She had gotten a few cute camping outfits in preparation for the trip, and she wasn't ready to part with any of her new things. "Can't we just make a small exception?" She batted her eyes at Mr. Gold as she waited for his reply.

"Sorry, Sharpay," Mr. Gold said, shaking his head. "There simply isn't room." He pointed to the large trunk at his feet. "What is in there, anyway?"

"Oh, that's my portable generator," Sharpay replied matter-of-factly.

"And why would you need that?" Mr. Gold inquired.

"For my hair dryer, of course!" Sharpay exclaimed. "I read there was no electricity, but that doesn't mean that I should have to sacrifice my hair quality, right?"

Mr. Gold shook his head again and took a deep breath. "Sharpay, you'll have to make some decisions and just take one bag. I suggest that you call your parents to come back to pick up the remaining luggage."

Sharpay harrumphed and pulled out her cell phone. "Mommy!" she cried into the phone. "I need to downsize quickly."

"Hey, Gabriella! Wait up!" Troy called as he spotted her at the door of the bus. He quickly jogged over, and they both climbed inside.

"Are you two ready for a great outdoor science adventure?" Ms. Darbus asked them.

"Yes," they said in unison. Laughing, they each settled into a seat and got comfortable for the long ride ahead.

Gabriella took a look around. Now that they were almost on their way, she was getting more and more excited. It would be so nice to spend some time with her friends, especially Troy, outside the school halls.

Finally, the bus pulled out of the parking lot, with everyone talking and cheering. But when they reached the highway, the noise lessened and soon many of the students had fallen asleep.

Even though Chad had worked hard to make a playlist for Taylor, they both nodded off before they could listen to a song. Sharpay, Ryan, Kelsi, and Ashley had drifted off, too. Even Jason and Zeke were fast asleep. But Gabriella and Troy couldn't sleep. They both sat huddled in their seats, thinking of ways to stump each other with lyrics to songs.

"I can't think of another song with the word gray," Troy said.

Gabriella sang a line from "You Are My Sunshine" with a grin on her face. It conveniently included the word gray.

"You're good at this game." Troy laughed. "You win that round."

"My mom and I used to play all the time on our car rides when we went camping," Gabriella confessed.

Troy laughed again. "Well, we'll see how well you do at pitching a tent," he joked with her.

"Troy Bolton, are you challenging me?" Gabriella teased. "Because I bet you that I can put up a tent faster than you."

Troy got a gleam in his blue eyes. "Oh, you're on, camper! I'd take that bet any day!"

CHAPTER THREE

When the bus rolled into the state park, it was close to lunchtime. Everyone piled out and followed Mr. Gold's directions to sit down at the picnic tables. Five rangers were standing in a row, ready to greet the Wildcats.

"Welcome, East High!" one of the rangers bellowed. "I'm Ranger Lou, and this is Ranger Jessica and Ranger Nicole." He pointed to the two rangers standing next to him. "And over there," he gestured to the two men standing off to his right, "are Ranger Andrew and Ranger Mike."

All the rangers waved hello.

"Ranger Mike is one hot ranger," Sharpay whispered to Ashley.

"Dreamy for sure," Ashley commented as she checked out the tall, tanned, blond ranger with bright green eyes. He was wearing beige shorts and a collared blue shirt with a state park emblem. Ashley sighed, fanning her face with her hand.

"We're here to make this an enjoyable and educational trip," Ranger Lou was saying. "We hope that you are respectful of our park, the animals, the land, and the water. And we hope that you will learn some valuable lessons while you are here."

"And have fun!" Ranger Mike added.

All the Wildcats whooped and hollered.

Mr. Gold stood up. "Thank you, rangers," he said. Then he turned to the group. "There are box lunches for you all over there on that table, so please line up to get them. After we eat, we set up camp. Then we'll meet back here at the picnic tables to break up into groups for the nature hike with the rangers."

"I want to be in Ranger Mike's group," Sharpay said, leaning over to Ashley.

"I think all the girls want to be on *his* team," Ashley noted as she looked around at the group. Most of the girls were talking and giggling amongst themselves.

Mr. Gold raised his arms to quiet the group. "And one more thing," he said. "We're going to have a scavenger hunt. I have broken up the class into two teams, blue and green. Kelsi Nielsen will be the captain of the blue team and Martha Cox will be the captain of the green team. The winning team will receive additional extra credit."

Kelsi and Martha both waved at the group. They looked a little embarrassed by all the attention, but happy to be chosen to lead the teams.

"I will pass out sheets with the team members' names and a checklist of different species of plants and birds, and other things pertaining to the ecosystems that we're studying here," Mr. Gold went on. "Your team will need to find *each* item if you want to get the extra credit."

Taylor was first in line for the scavenger-hunt sheet. Grabbing it, she joined her friends at the tables. She scanned the list and smiled. "Gabriella!" she cried. "We're both on Kelsi's team!"

"Me, too," Chad said, checking out the list between bites of his sandwich. "But, bummer, Troy, you're on Martha's team."

Gabriella couldn't help but be a little disappointed that Troy wasn't on her team. She had hoped to spend the whole weekend with him.

"Don't worry, Troy," Ashley said, walking up with a flirtatious smile on her face. She put her arm around Troy. "Sharpay and I are on Martha's team. We'll keep you company."

Taylor leaned over to Gabriella. "I bet they will," she said through gritted teeth.

A small smile spread across Gabriella's face.

She was not about to let Sharpay or Ashley bother her. She had a more important competition on her mind. Throwing out the remains of her boxed lunch, she looked over at Troy. "Let the tent-raising begin!" she exclaimed. "Are you ready for that challenge, Mr. Bolton?"

Troy laughed. "Oh, yeah," he said. "You get your tent mates, and I'll get mine."

"You're on!" Gabriella told him.

Taylor, Kelsi, and Sharpay were all assigned to Gabriella's tent. Quickly, Gabriella and Kelsi went to get the tent from Ranger Lou while Taylor found a good, level spot. Sharpay, however, flounced over to sit on the picnic table to talk to Ranger Mike.

"Looks like Sharpay isn't going to be joining us," Gabriella said to Kelsi as they walked past her.

"I don't think she'd be much help, anyway," Kelsi said. "Maybe it's better this way."

At the same time, Troy was gathering his tent supplies with Chad, Ryan, and Timothy

Martin. Each of them grabbed some poles.

"No beds, huh?" Ryan summarized as he looked around. "Sleeping on the ground is not very ergonomic. I need good support for my back." He raised up his arms to do a slow stretch, for emphasis.

"You'll be fine," Chad told him as he grabbed a blanket. "It's only a few nights."

"Come on, guys," Troy said, trying to move his tent mates along. "We have to beat the girls. We can do this tent thing."

But Troy was in for a surprise. The tents were similar to the one that Gabriella had assembled with her mother many times before. She quickly rolled out the tent and handed out the stakes to Taylor and Kelsi.

"Make sure to put the stakes in at an angle," she advised. Then she slipped the long poles through the holes on the top of the tent. As she did, she glanced over at Troy and his group. Their tent was still in the bag on the ground. She smiled.

"Where do these go?" Chad asked, holding up a bag of small stakes.

"In the ground?" Ryan guessed. He scratched his head and then straightened his orange cap.

Troy shook his head. "Haven't you guys ever gone camping?" He pulled the tent out of the bag and rolled it out on the ground. "Come on, let's get going. Gabriella and the girls are almost finished. We've got to hustle." He quickly pushed the long poles through the top loops on the tent.

"I think you forgot something," Timothy said. He was standing off to the side, holding the tent instructions in his hand.

"What?" Troy asked. "We have everything here. Come on, team, let's move!" Troy worked fast and pulled the cords tight to lift up the tent. As it popped up, Troy stood back, ready to gloat at Gabriella.

Just then, the wind blew and picked up the boys' tent, carrying it down the hill.

"You forgot," Timothy said, finally finishing his thought, "to stake the tent." He looked up from the page of instructions long enough to see that the tent was gone. "It says here that the first thing to do is to put the stakes in the ground at an angle to secure the tent."

"Need some help?" Gabriella called.

Troy looked over to see Gabriella, Taylor, and Kelsi holding his flyaway tent. He had to smile.

"I guess we *could* use your help," Troy said, defeated. "You definitely won that one, hands down."

"*Tent* down is more like it," Taylor said, with a wide grin.

"We got blown away," Troy responded with a smile.

They all laughed, as together, the girls helped the boys secure their tent to the ground.

"Ah, home, sweet home," Ryan sang as he climbed inside a few moments later.

"Come on," Zeke said, running by. "People are gathering back at the picnic tables for the hiking groups."

As the others rushed off, Troy looked over at Gabriella. "Thanks," he said. Then he grabbed her hand. "Come on, let's go see some nature."

CHAPTER FOUR

Mr. Gold was speaking to the group when Troy and Gabriella arrived at the picnic tables. They joined their friends and took seats. "Please give your attention to Ms. Darbus," Mr. Gold said. "We're so lucky to have her here on this trip with us, and she has planned a very special event for you on our last night that I'm sure you will enjoy."

Ms. Darbus stood up, straightening her sweatsuit jacket. She looked around at the students, gave a dramatic pause, and began to speak. "Thank you, Mr. Gold," she said sweetly. "I have indeed planned a special evening for our last night here. Since we will be outdoors under the stars on this beautiful land, I think that it would be lovely to have a traditional Native American storytelling event. Similar to what might have occurred on these grounds many years ago, we will be gathering for a bonfire."

"Awesome!" Jason exclaimed. "Maybe we'll toast marshmallows, too."

Ms. Darbus gave Jason a stern look. "Don't worry, Jason," she said. "There will be plenty of time for that. I would like you all to come up with stories that will be acted out and shared with the group."

"Or perhaps stories that are put to music?" Sharpay asked. She flashed her teacher a full smile and then winked at Ryan. The Evanses were always ready for a performance.

Ms. Darbus grinned at her prized student. "Why, that would be lovely!" the teacher said enthusiastically. "I was able to borrow a traditional Native American talking stick that we will pass around to make the evening truly authentic. The talking stick was traditionally used at council meetings and whoever had the stick had the right to speak."

"I've read about that," Taylor said. "It gave each member of the council time to speak and be heard at tribal meetings. There are spiritual qualities to the stick, too."

"That is correct," Ms. Darbus said to Taylor. "We're going to use the stick more for the story-telling, but the same principles of use will apply."

"As if some people around here really need to have a stick to help them talk," Chad whispered to Troy.

Troy laughed, and nodded in agreement. "I bet Sharpay and Ryan have a whole sound system ready."

"Anyway, if you would like to share a story, that would be wonderful," Ms. Darbus contin-ued. "Please come find me and let me know if you'd like to participate, or we can be spontaneous that evening. I am hoping that many of you will share your talents and our last evening here will be a memorable event."

"Do ghost stories count?" Chad called out.

Ms. Darbus made a sour face. "Well, that is not what I had in mind, Chad," she said. "There will be time for that sort of storytelling at tonight's bonfire, I am sure."

Mr. Gold nodded his head, confirming that ghost stories were on the agenda for the night's activities.

"Cool," Chad said. "Because I have a *howling* good one!"

Jason laughed and hit a high five with Chad. Then they both howled like crazed werewolves.

"All right, students," Mr. Gold said. "Our rangers are here and ready to help us explore the trails. There is a lot to learn out here so keep your eyes open."

Everyone was well aware of the five rangers standing at the front, serious expressions on their faces. The rangers nodded along with Mr. Gold.

"There are several items on your scavenger-hunt list that you might run across," Mr. Gold went on. "So be sure to keep your eyes open. Each hiking group has members of the blue team and members of the green team. So work with each other." Then he looked around at his students. "And please, stick together. These trails that we're exploring are winding, and they snake deep into the woods."

"Did you say snakes?" Ami Jones, one of East High's cheerleaders, squealed. A few other girls screamed as well.

Ranger Lou stepped forward. He put his hands up to quiet the crowd. "Don't worry about snakes," he said. "Just be aware and remain alert out on the trails. You are visitors here and need to be respectful of the wildlife that lives in the woods."

"I just hope those snakes respect *my* space!" Chad called out.

Everyone laughed and then started to move toward their assigned ranger.

Sharpay and Ashley floated over to Ranger Mike, happy to be in his group. They suddenly had a great interest in, and motivation for, studying nature and science.

Gabriella and Kelsi exchanged a look.

"I have a feeling this is going to be a long hike," Kelsi lamented. She and Gabriella were in Ranger Mike's group as well.

"Well, like Mr. Gold said, we can get a head start on our scavenger list," Gabriella offered, holding up the sheet of paper for the blue team. "We're bound to see some of these plants and trees on the hike, so keep a look out."

"Clearly, not everyone is going to be watching out for that," Taylor said with a smirk as she watched Sharpay and Ashley batting their eyes at Ranger Mike. "I'm glad those girls aren't on our team. It gives us a definite advantage."

Just then Chad jogged up to Taylor. "See you later," he said. Chad had been assigned to

Ranger Nicole's group while Troy and Jason were in Ranger Lou's.

"See ya," Taylor replied. Then she said good-bye to Gabriella and Kelsi and made her way over to join Ranger Andrew's group.

Taylor quickly took note of the other blue-team members in her group. She saw Ami and two of her cheerleader friends, Lisa Williams and Danielle McClements, and Ryan. Taylor sighed. She'd have to pay extraclose attention on the walk. She doubted the others would be as aware. And she'd have to be careful; the captain of the green team, Martha, was in her group, too.

"Come this way," Ranger Andrew said. "We'll go down by the lake and up the south trail." He looked around at the students.

Taylor stepped in behind Ranger Andrew. She wanted to be the first to see everything.

"Do you think we'll spot an owl's nest or even a rattlesnake?" Taylor asked the ranger.

"Rattlesnake!" Ami cried. She opened her

mouth to scream and her two friends joined in to make the sound in stereo.

Ranger Andrew covered his ears and looked at the girls sternly. "No need to worry about that," he said calmly. "And no reason to scream. As Ranger Lou told you, we need to respect the woods and the wildlife that live here." Then he looked at Ami and her friends sternly. "Not to mention my eardrums."

The cheerleaders nodded their heads and agreed to be quiet as the group explored the trail. As they walked along, Ranger Andrew pointed to trees and birds' nests. When they got to one particularly large shrub, the ranger stopped. "Big sagebrush is one of the most widely known shrubs of the Southwest."

"It smells pretty bad," Martha said, getting up close enough to smell the pungent odor.

"Actually, Native Americans often used the plant to help neutralize the effects of strong odors, such as that of a skunk," Ranger Andrew told the students.

As he continued to talk, Taylor noticed a desert cottontail sitting in the shade of a bush. She checked her scavenger-hunt list and, sure enough, the animal was on it. She didn't want to say anything because there were green team members standing next to her. And she knew they had not noticed the furry little creature. As inconspicuously as possible, she leaned over to Ryan, and pointed to the rabbit and the list.

Ryan squinted at the bush and nodded. He hung back while Ranger Andrew moved on to show the group a tall tree by the edge of the trail.

"I bet if we get a picture of that rabbit, Mr. Gold will give us bonus points," Taylor whispered to Ryan.

"My cell phone has a camera," he offered. Just as he was about to pull the phone out of his pocket, the rabbit jumped out from the shade and went under another bush.

"Oh, no," Taylor said. Her competitive spirit

was heating up. "Come on, Ryan," she urged. "You can still get the picture if you get a little closer."

Ryan took off his cap and wiped his forehead. "No problem," he said.

Taylor looked over her shoulder to see where Ranger Andrew was standing. He was pointing to some tall trees with his back to Taylor. All the other students had their backs turned as well and were unaware of Ryan and Taylor's mission. Now was their chance.

"Hurry up!" Taylor called to Ryan in a low whisper. "I'll watch Ranger Andrew, you get the picture."

The small bunny continued to hop from shrub to shrub. Ryan hopped, too. He leaped over tree stumps and rocks to keep the rabbit in view, but he couldn't seem to get close enough to capture the image.

"Oh, let me do it!" Taylor huffed as she grew more and more impatient. She stomped over and took the phone from Ryan. Standing on a rock, she leaned in to get the rabbit and its twitching ears into the photo.

Click!

"I got it!" Taylor exclaimed. She turned with a proud smile on her face, ready to gloat to Martha and the rest of the green team members in the group.

But no one was there.

Ryan shook his head. He looked around at the eerily empty trail. "I think that you got us lost," he said. "You were supposed to be watching which way Ranger Andrew went while I followed the rabbit."

"Oh, Ryan, he clearly went this way," Taylor said, slightly annoyed. She pointed to the trail to the right. But it looked very quiet and still. "Or maybe it was this way?" She peered down the trail to the left. "Um, actually, I don't know."

Ryan shook his head. "You don't know?" He put his hands on his hips. "Taylor, you *always* know the right answer."

She shrugged her shoulders. "Well, this time

I don't," she replied. She felt her heart start to race.

"Well, what good is the picture of the rabbit," Ryan asked, "if we can't get back to camp?" His voice escalated to a higher octave as he got more nervous.

"Oh, come on," Taylor told him, trying to ignore Ryan's drama-king outburst that matched her own inner freak-out. She tried to think positively. "We can't be too far behind. How fast could they all walk? Let's go this way." She pointed to the right. "I think I see footprints over there by the flat rock."

Following Taylor, Ryan kept his eyes on the ground in front of him. He didn't want to step on any rattlesnakes. After about ten minutes, there was still no sign of Ranger Andrew and the rest of their group. Ryan stopped walking.

"I think we are now officially lost," Ryan said with a sigh. He sat down on a fallen tree log and opened his phone. "No signal," he moaned. "And it's going to get dark soon."

Taylor looked back at him. "Don't be silly," she said. "I am sure that the group is just up ahead, let's keep moving."

"There are bears that live here, you know," Ryan whined. He looked around cautiously.

Taylor pulled up Ryan and trudged on. But after fifteen more minutes, even Taylor was beginning to feel a bit disheartened. There was still no one in sight.

How could a loud group of teenagers and a ranger disappear so fast?

CHAPTER FIVE

Sharpay was not about to let Ranger Mike out of her sight. She was right by his side as he described the types of trees that surrounded her group out on the forest trail.

"You can identify a Southwestern Ponderosa Pine by its two to three long needles," the ranger stated, pointing at one of the trees. "It can grow to be about one-hundred-fifty-feet tall and the immature cones are green in color."

"Wow!" Sharpay gushed. She stepped closer

to Ranger Mike. She flipped her blonde hair and then gave him a wide smile.

Ashley, on his other side, was also listening intently to his speech. "So tall and strong," she said in a dreamy voice.

Kelsi, meanwhile, stood off to the side, trying hard not to roll her eyes. She couldn't believe those girls were acting like Ranger Mike was some kind of television superstar. She shot Gabriella a knowing look.

"How old is this one?" Sharpay asked, hoping to get Ranger Mike to turn his full attention to her for a moment.

Ranger Mike considered the tree. "This one here is probably around two hundred years old."

"Beautiful," Sharpay whispered.

"Let's keep moving," Ranger Mike said, encouraging his group on. "Come this way, but please watch your step."

As the group filed carefully along the narrow trail, Sharpay saw a perfect opportunity to get a bit more attention from Ranger Mike. All her acting training was about to come in handy.

Letting out a squeal, she feigned tripping over a stone and stumbled to the ground. "Ouch!" she moaned.

Ranger Mike spun around. "Are you all right?" he asked, springing into action.

As he moved to help Sharpay up, Ashley fumed. Sharpay had outsmarted her. Why didn't she think of twisting her ankle!

Like an emergency room doctor, he put his hands on Sharpay's ankle to assess the damage. "Does this hurt?"

"A little," Sharpay said in a quiet voice.

"How about this?" Ranger Mike asked, pressing down on a different spot.

"I'll help her the rest of the way," Ashley offered, interrupting the medical examination. There was no way she was going to let Sharpay get Ranger Mike's arm on her shoulder for the rest of the nature walk.

"That's being a good friend," Ranger Mike said approvingly. "Sharpay, can you handle the walk back? You're a trooper, right?"

Sharpay couldn't say no. "I'll be able to manage," she said softly. "I don't want to miss a thing."

"Great," Ranger Mike said. "You stay next to Ashley, and we'll keep going, then."

Sharpay smiled at Ranger Mike, but once he turned around she glared at Ashley. "Don't even think about touching me," she hissed through clenched teeth.

"Oh, my, what a miraculous recovery!" Ashley exclaimed.

Defeated, Sharpay huffed and followed the rest of the group, limping the entire way.

As the hiking groups made their way off the trails and back to the campsite, they congregated at the picnic tables. People were buzzing about items they had found on the hike that were on the scavenger-hunt list.

Martha and Kelsi were at the center of the two crowds that were beginning to form—the green and blue teams.

Martha cheered as her team circled around her. Everyone was handing her samples and reports from their hikes. "Great work!" she gushed.

Over on the other side of the camp, Kelsi scanned her clipboard with items already checked off and looked up at her team. "Good job, guys!" She was really impressed with how everyone was working together. It felt good to be the leader of something. Usually she was in the wings or hidden behind sheet music. She hoped she'd be able to handle the responsibility as the competition started to heat up.

All the other groups had returned by the time Chad's group made it back to the site. The other Wildcats were hanging out around the picnic tables, chatting and relaxing. Chad searched the area looking for Taylor. When he didn't see her, he walked over to Martha.

"Where's Taylor?" he asked. "Wasn't she in your hiking group?"

Martha shrugged. "She was with Ryan. Aren't they here?" She looked around. "I just assumed they were ahead of me on the trail."

Chad started moving through the crowd of students as if he were dribbling a basketball down center court. "Taylor? Has anyone seen Taylor?" he asked anxiously.

Kelsi pushed her glasses up on her nose and looked around. She and Gabriella had met with Troy and Jason after the hikes and were lounging at one of the picnic tables. "It's not like Taylor to not follow directions," Kelsi observed. "She knew that we were all supposed to be back here at the picnic tables."

"Martha said Ryan and Taylor were together," Gabriella added. "And Ryan's always on time." She turned to scan the crowd of students. "Do you think that they're lost?"

Before anyone could answer, Chad came running up to his friends. "It's getting dark.

Taylor is out there in the dangerous woods! We have to do something!" He dragged his hands through his curly brown hair. His eyes were wide and full of panic.

Troy reached out to Chad, grabbing his shoulder. "Chill, Chad. I'm sure that Taylor is okay. She's a smart girl."

"Yeah, but she isn't a smart *outdoor* girl," Chad said. "Man, you heard Ranger Lou. There are bears and rattlesnakes out there."

"He didn't say anything about bears," Gabriella said, trying her best to calm down Chad. "We shouldn't jump to conclusions."

"Probably because he didn't want to scare everyone," Jason added.

Gabriella gave Jason a look. He was *not* helping.

"Listen," Chad said frantically. "I've seen all these movies about people who get lost in the woods. They don't come back! They NEVER come back!"

"Okay, hold on," Troy said, ever the leader.

"Let's get organized. We can gather a group to go look for them. Teamwork, remember?"

"Good idea. But first, let's go tell Mr. Gold and Ranger Lou," Gabriella offered.

The two men were not happy to hear the news. Ranger Lou quickly went to speak with Ranger Andrew, hoping he might have some more information. But the ranger was as surprised as everyone else that two students from his group were missing.

"I was sure that everyone was behind me," the apologetic ranger explained. "I'll go back and search right away."

"We can help you," Troy said, standing with his friends.

Mr. Gold put a hand on Troy's back. "I don't need more than two students wandering around the trails as the sun sets," he said. "The rangers can handle this."

With no other choice, Chad, Troy, Jason, Gabriella, and Kelsi went to sit at a picnic table off to the side. A few minutes later, Zeke joined them.

"This is crazy," Chad said, pulling again at his hair. He was too hyper to sit down. He began pacing around the table as if he were doing laps in the gym. "They should let us help."

"The rangers know what they're doing," Gabriella said again. The truth was that she was getting nervous about Taylor and Ryan being out in the woods alone, too.

The sun was starting to slip down below the tall row of trees, and Gabriella shivered. The air was getting colder, and the sun had almost set. She hoped that the rangers would be able to find Taylor and Ryan quickly. The forest was no place to be after dark.

CHAPTER SIX

"Uh, Taylor," Ryan said. "I'm pretty sure we are walking in circles."

Turning around to face Ryan, Taylor pursed her lips. "What? We are not, Ryan. Let's keep moving."

Ryan pointed to the tree log in front of him. "I sat on this log about a half hour ago," he said. "Remember?"

"Oh, no! Ryan, you're right!" Taylor cried. Suddenly, the full weight of the situation hit her.

She sat down on the ground and cradled her head in her hands.

"I wouldn't do that," Ryan told her.

"What?" Taylor snapped. "Sit down? We've been walking forever. We're lost! And it's getting dark fast."

Pointing to the spot where Taylor was sitting, Ryan said, "No, I meant I wouldn't do *that*. You are sitting in poison oak."

"I am not," Taylor shot back. "Everyone knows poison oak looks like . . ." She looked down at the ground where she was sitting, where she had just placed her hands, and stopped talking. She took a deep breath. "Just perfect," she mumbled. "Lost, and soon to be itchy."

"Where's Ryan?" Sharpay demanded, charging up to Gabriella, Troy, and their friends. She had given up limping already since that didn't get her much mileage with Ranger Mike and proved a hard act to keep up. "Has anyone seen my brother? I've been looking for him all over."

"Well, so has everyone else," Chad said. "Except us."

Sharpay looked at Chad, her brown eyes squinting in confusion. "What are you talking about?"

"Taylor and Ryan didn't come back with their group," Zeke explained, trying to sound calm and comforting. He didn't want Sharpay to get upset about her missing brother.

For a moment, Sharpay looked genuinely worried and her hand went to her heart. But then Troy piped up.

"The rangers are all looking for them now," he said reassuringly.

"They should be back any minute," Gabriella added.

The look of worry disappeared. "But I need Ryan *now*!" Sharpay whined loudly. "Where is he?" She stomped her foot in the dirt. "I can't find the key for my suitcase. He has the spare keys to my luggage. He better be back by the time I am out of the shower." Then she turned and ran off to change out of her dirty hiking clothes.

Troy watched her stalk off. I guess we know what really matters to Sharpay, he thought to himself. Or, maybe she's just hiding her real feelings.

"She's so distraught about the news," Zeke said, as if in answer to Troy's musings. "Poor, worried thing."

"Oh, please," Gabriella moaned. Zeke was way too smitten. But even if Sharpay wasn't outwardly concerned, Gabriella was. Where were her friends?

Ryan sat across from Taylor on a rock. He closed his eyes and took a deep, cleansing breath. "It helps to breathe," he said. "Right before I go onstage, I always do that, and it calms my nerves."

Taylor tried to imitate Ryan's breathing technique, but she didn't feel calmer. She scratched her hands. She knew poison oak took a while to spread, but she already had phantom itching all over her body.

"Taylor," Ryan said, sounding irritatingly calm. "This is like the time when Sharpay and I had to sing for the spring musical a couple of years ago without any microphones. We just had to power through."

Taylor looked up at Ryan in complete disbelief.

"No one thought that we could pull off the show," Ryan continued, "but we did. We did because we had to." He clapped his hands. "Come on, Taylor. You gotta get up and try. We can find our way out of here."

"Ryan, this isn't a musical! We're lost in the forest," Taylor said. "There's no cell coverage, no one probably knows we're gone. Ranger Andrew can't have realized we are missing or else he would have come back for us."

Ryan's eyes scanned the sky thoughtfully. "The sun sets in the west so let's go that way." He pointed behind them, where the sun was sinking below the horizon. "When we started walking with Ranger Andrew the sun was in my eyes, so camp must be back that way."

Speechless, Taylor got up and stared at Ryan. "Wow, that was really impressive," she said after a moment. "I never would have thought that I'd be saying this, but I'm really glad that you are on the blue team. And that you're here now."

Ryan blushed uncharacteristically. "Thanks," he said. "I appreciate that."

"Now," said Taylor, rejuvenated, "let's try to get back to camp, shall we?"

"Where are they?" Chad shouted for what felt like the thousandth time. He finally stopped pacing and sat down on the bench next to Troy.

Gabriella put her hand on Chad's back. "We're all nervous about them, Chad, but the rangers know these trails well. I'm sure they will find them."

The sun was sinking quickly now and had turned the sky into a mesh of reds and oranges.

Ms. Darbus walked over with some lanterns for each of the picnic tables. If she hadn't been so nervous, Gabriella would have found the whole scene quite beautiful, not to mention incredibly romantic.

"They'll be back soon," Ms. Darbus said, noticing the students' concerned expressions. "Worrying isn't going to help."

"No," Chad said. "But sitting here doing nothing doesn't help, either."

Taylor looked down at her once-white shirt and pressed khaki shorts. She was now covered in dirt, her clothes were all wrinkled, and her hands and face were definitely starting to itch. On top of all that, she was tired and hungry.

"This seems useless," Taylor said, sitting down on the ground. Her earlier excitement about Ryan's logic had disappeared. "Maybe we should just wait here for someone to find us. They must have realized by now that we're lost, right? You don't think the rangers have already given up do you?" Her voice squeaked and she felt tears threaten.

"Don't give up!" Ryan demanded. He was determined to get back to the campsite. He could totally use a long, hot shower.

"This is just a disaster," Taylor moaned. "We should never have left the group."

"But we did get the picture of the desert cottontail," Ryan pointed out. "The blue team is going to be happy about that."

"If we ever get back to tell anyone," Taylor mumbled.

At that moment, there was a rustling sound in a bush near Taylor's foot. She jumped up and moved far away from the shrub.

"What was that?" she yelled.

"I don't know and don't want to find out," Ryan said, scooting away. "Let's keep walking."

Taylor followed Ryan. She hugged her arms around her chest, hoping that they'd see some friendly faces soon.

* * *

Sharpay stomped over to the picnic area in a pink chenille robe and white fuzzy slippers. "Ryan still isn't back?"

Chad shook his head. "No sign. No word." He was so distressed he didn't even notice Sharpay's apparel.

"Well, where are the rangers?" she asked. "Where is Ranger Mike?"

Ms. Darbus came over and put an arm around Sharpay. She had mistaken the girl's tantrum for concern. "They haven't been gone that long," she said. "I am sure that everyone will be back long before dinner."

"You mean he really is lost?" Sharpay whispered, her voice now full of concern. She turned on her fuzzy slipper heels and looked around at all the Wildcats.

Ms. Darbus walked Sharpay over to a table to sit down and wait. "Don't worry, dear," she said. "He'll be back before you know it."

"She's really torn up, huh?" Zeke asked sincerely.

Gabriella nodded. Sharpay didn't appear to be acting—which made Gabriella even more worried.

Ryan looked up at the sky. "Mr. Gold was right. It is pretty nice here," he said. "Just look at that." He pointed to the glowing horizon in front of them.

"It looks like a painting," Taylor noted. Even though her stomach was twisted up with nerves, she had to admit that the scene before her was pretty amazing.

"A Monet painting," Ryan said.

Once again Ryan surprised Taylor. "Claude Monet, the famous French Impressionist painter?" Taylor replied. "Ryan, you like Impressionism?"

"A lot, actually," he said. "My parents drag me and Sharpay to art museums all the time. I kind of like the Impressionist stuff the best."

"Wow, I never knew that about you. That's really cool." Taylor looked up at the sky. Then she smiled at Ryan. Maybe getting lost wasn't completely awful. If they hadn't, she'd never have known there was more to Ryan than his hats and dramatic stage presence.

Now, if we could only find our way back to camp, Taylor wished as she and Ryan continued on their trek, I could enjoy the bonding even more.

CHAPTER SEVEN

It was dinnertime, and Taylor and Ryan were still missing in action. The Wildcats assigned for dinner duty were chopping and cooking the meal. But no one was saying very much. Everyone was worried.

Chad was no longer pacing; he was now sitting quietly and rubbing his hands together. "It's getting really cold," he said to Gabriella. "Taylor and Ryan are probably freezing out there."

Nodding, Gabriella agreed with Chad. "Let's

keep hoping for the best," she said. "Maybe they'll make it back before dinner is on the table." Giving Chad one more reassuring look, she got up to get a sweater from her tent.

Zeke was very worried, too. So he was doing what he always did in times of crisis—he was baking. He was now busy preparing brownies for everyone. It was a little tricky because he was using long pans that sat on a grate above the fire instead of in a conventional oven. As he positioned his pans on the fire, he saw Gabriella walking up to her tent alone. Now was his chance to get some valuable—and much needed—Gabriella advice.

"Hey, Gabriella!" Zeke called, jogging to catch up with her. "Can I talk to you for a minute?"

"Sure," Gabriella said. "What's up?"

Falling in step with her, Zeke lowered his voice to make his confession. "I think I made a huge mistake," he said. He looked down at the ground as he spoke. "And now I don't know how to get out of it."

Gabriella stopped walking and faced Zeke. "What do you mean?"

"I kinda, maybe, might have led Sharpay to believe that I'm a really good horseback rider," he said, looking up to meet her gaze. "And, um, I'm not."

Raising her eyebrows, Gabriella just stared at Zeke.

"I know," he said. "Pretty dumb. The truth is, horses and I, well, we don't really get along. We're sort of like oil and water."

"Oh, Zeke," Gabriella sympathized. She put a hand on his shoulder. "I overheard Ranger Jessica talking about the horse ride. There are two trails, and the expert one sounds pretty advanced."

"That was what I was afraid of," Zeke said, kicking at a rock by his foot.

"You have to say something to Sharpay," Gabriella urged. "Otherwise you'll end up on the wrong trail. Why don't you tell her after dinner tonight?"

Zeke sighed. Gabriella makes telling Sharpay the truth sound easier than it would be, he thought. Her words ringing in his ears, he headed back to check on his brownies. But suddenly, he wasn't very hungry.

No one really ate much at dinner. And instead of the usual level of noise at a meal, there was a quiet hush over the campground.

Mr. Gold got up to speak to the group. "Clearly, we are all concerned about Taylor and Ryan," he said. "But there is a search party out looking for them now. Please try to think good thoughts and continue to cooperate with the rangers."

"This is ridiculous," Sharpay sniped, walking by to throw out her untouched plate of food.

"You must be so worried about Ryan," Kelsi said to her. She was sure that Sharpay was feeling badly about Ryan's disappearance.

"Worried?" Sharpay said with a pout. "Of course, I'm worried. Have you noticed that all

73

the rangers are out on the trails searching for him? *And*, I still haven't gotten to take my shower," she added half-heartedly.

Kelsi backed away from Sharpay and slinked over to her table, where Gabriella, Troy, and Chad were sitting. "Gee," Kelsi said. "Sharpay is more upset than I realized. Or, she is putting on a good act."

Gabriella glanced over at Sharpay. "She does look a bit unraveled," she said, noticing that Sharpay was still in her bathrobe with a towel wrapped around her head.

"Let's hope that the search party finds them soon," Troy said. "At least there's a full moon out tonight so there will be light if they have to keep searching when the sun goes down."

"A full moon means werewolves," Jason added.

"JASON!" they all shouted. Once again, his humor was not helping to calm anyone's nerves, especially Chad's.

* * *

"I'm starving," Ryan whined. "What do you think they are serving back at the campsite for dinner?"

"I don't know," Taylor answered. "But I sure hope that we get to camp before they clear all the food away."

Ryan sat down on a rock. "Let's just sit for a second," he said.

Taking a seat next to him, Taylor sighed. "We really should keep moving. I'd hate to be out here all night, ya know?"

"Especially with a full moon on the rise," Ryan said, pointing up to the sky. Already, he could see the moon coming up over the horizon. It wouldn't be long until it was true night. . . .

Standing up, Taylor brushed off the dirt from her legs. Then she stretched. As she stood on her toes, she caught a glimpse of something. "Look, over there, behind those trees!" she cried. "I think I see our camp!"

Letting out excited yelps, Taylor and Ryan ran

down the sloped trail. In moments, they burst into the camp.

"There they are!" shouted Troy as Taylor and Ryan came into view. "Mr. Gold! Mr. Gold! They're here!"

Chad was the first to reach them. Taylor put her hand up to block Chad.

"Don't touch me!" she cried. "I have poison oak!"

Chad looked hurt. That was not the greeting he had expected. He backed away.

"Poison oak?!" Gabriella cried out. She had had that once and felt bad for her soon-to-be very-itchy friend. "What happened to you guys?"

"Everyone was worried," Troy put in.

"Especially Chad," Jason told them, giving Chad a friendly punch in the arm.

Mr. Gold ran over to the crowd. He was relieved to see Taylor and Ryan, and welcomed them back. But when that was over, he launched into a stern lecture about staying with the adult supervisor and paying attention to the rules of the trip.

When he was finished, Ryan explained how he and Taylor saw a desert cottontail and wanted to get a picture. "Then we lost sight of Ranger Andrew and the group," he said.

"But Ryan figured out which way camp was by looking at the setting sun," Taylor told everyone.

Ryan blushed. While it was nice to get the credit, he felt a little embarrassed. Then he turned to Mr. Gold. "We didn't miss dinner, did we? Is there any food left?"

"Yes, of course," Mr. Gold said. "In fact, you and Taylor will be on cleanup duty for the meal. That is, after you assure me that you have learned your lesson."

"Oh, we have," Taylor and Ryan said. "No more roaming around off the marked trails, that's for sure!"

"And that you will follow directions when you go out on a trail again," Mr. Gold said.

Both Taylor and Ryan nodded their heads.

Mr. Gold radioed the rangers who were still out on the trails and told them that the two

Wildcats had returned to camp safe and sound. "We've got them here," he said into the receiver. "Come on back for dinner."

Just then, Sharpay rushed up to Ryan. Her white towel was still twisted around her head, and her pink chenille robe and fuzzy slippers were a bit worse for the wear. "Thank goodness you're back!" Sharpay exclaimed. She gave Ryan a long hug, squeezing him tightly.

Touched that his sister cared so much, Ryan blushed again. "Well, I—" he started to say before Sharpay cut him off. Now that he was back safely, she had issues to resolve.

"I need the extra key for my suitcase right now!" Sharpay demanded. "I've been waiting all night to get some conditioner in my hair!"

Ryan rolled his eyes and dug into his pocket to produce the key for his sister.

After all the pots and plates were washed, dried, and put away, Taylor and Ryan joined their classmates at the bonfire. Everyone else had already gathered, and they were now sitting around telling ghost stories.

When Taylor and Ryan walked up, Chad was in the middle of a particularly gruesome tale. Taylor surveyed the circle. Sharpay was sitting next to Ranger Mike in her canvas folding chair. Ashley was next to her, trying to hone in on Sharpay's conversation with the ranger. Taylor shook her head and kept walking around the circle, looking for an empty seat. She was feeling a bit swollen and itchy. She hoped that the ointment Ranger Lou had given her at dinner would help.

Finally, she saw Gabriella sharing a blanket with Troy. They both moved over so Taylor could sit down.

"I am the ghost with the bloody finger!" Chad moaned in his spookiest voice. He switched on his flashlight and placed the light under his chin. His face glowed. "I am the ghost with the bloody finger!" he cried again and hobbled around the circle as if he were in a great deal of pain. He quickly turned and approached Taylor, surprising her by suddenly sticking out his finger. "Do you have a bandage?" he asked in a supersweet voice.

Everyone in the circle laughed—except for Taylor who was not in the mood to be scared or laughed at. Wasn't it enough that she had been humiliated already by getting lost? And that she was now covered in poison oak? She got up and stormed off to her tent.

"Hey, Taylor!" Chad called. "Come on! That was a good one!" Watching Taylor run off, he wondered what had made her so angry.

His head spinning, Chad sat down next to Jason and Zeke. He let out a loud sigh. Maybe tomorrow he'd have better luck with Taylor. At least he hoped so.

Then Ranger Mike stood up to take a turn. "I have a story that is a legend in these parts," he said. "It is a tale about a beloved and respected chief of a tribe of Native Americans who lived in these foothills many years ago."

Everyone grew very quiet as Ranger Mike walked slowly around the circle, making sure that he had everyone's attention before he began his tale.

"The Chief's closest companion was an old coyote with one eye," Ranger Mike went on. "Many were afraid of the one-eyed coyote, but the chief never went anywhere without him. When he hunted and even when he slept, the old coyote was next to him."

Sharpay and Ashley leaned in closer to the circle as Ranger Mike spoke. His hushed voice made the story even more compelling.

"The chief was very kind to all animals, but especially to all the coyotes who roamed the mountains. It was said that he would often leave food for them in the winter months. One day, when he and the one-eyed coyote were hunting up in the northern trails high up on the mountain, there was a disastrous avalanche." Pausing, Mike pointed up to the northern part of the mountain.

As if on cue, the wind blew, rustling the leaves

in the trees surrounding the campfire. Gabriella snuggled closer to Troy. She was glad that she was sitting next to him, with his arm securely around her.

"The snow rolled quickly down the mountain, burying everything in sight," Ranger Mike continued. "After the snow settled, the tribe realized the chief—and the coyote—had disappeared. They were never seen again. It was a great tragedy for the tribe, and some people say the chief and the coyote still roam the trails. When you hear the howls from the mountains, it's the ghost of the old one-eyed coyote, mourning his lost life."

Hoooowwwwwwwwwwwl. Hoooowwwwwwwwwwwl. Hoooowwwwwwwwwwwl.

The lonely sound of a coyote echoed through the campsite, startling even Ranger Mike.

The group around the fire screamed and then dissolved into nervous laughter.

"Okay, let's wrap it up," Ms. Darbus said, glancing at her watch and shooting her own nervous look at the mountain. "We've got a big day tomorrow."

"Come on, everyone," Mr. Gold echoed. "Let's get a good night's rest."

Troy stood up. "I didn't get to tell my story!"

"I think we've had enough scares for the night," Mr. Gold told him.

Reluctantly, Troy got up and helped Gabriella fold the blanket they had been sitting on. She turned to look for her tent mates.

Hoooowwwwwwwwwl. Hoooowwwwwwwwl. Hoooowwwwwl.

"Troy, that's not funny," Gabriella said. "Don't try to scare us."

"I didn't do it," Troy said. He held up his hands innocently. "Honest."

Gabriella looked over at Chad and Jason, the two greatest practical jokesters in their school.

"Wasn't us," Chad said before Gabriella could say anything.

Hoooowwwwwwwwwl. Hoooowwwwwwwwl. Hoooowwwwwl.

It sounded like the cries were coming closer!

Everyone stopped walking and looked around.

"Seriously, Troy," Gabriella said. "You're scaring me."

"I swear it wasn't me," Troy said. And this time, Gabriella believed him because his face seemed to mirror the same concern as the rest of the Wildcats.

Up ahead, Ranger Mike waved his flashlight. "Don't worry," he called. "That's just the coyote's way of saying good night."

"That's easy for him to say," Kelsi whispered to Gabriella. "He isn't sleeping in a tent!"

"Come on," Gabriella said to her friends. "Let's get inside."

"I'm with you on that," Zeke said as he sprinted up to his tent.

"Good night, guys!" Gabriella called.

"See you tomorrow," Troy said, giving Gabriella a wink. Then he leaned in and whispered in her ear. "See you later, okay?"

Gabriella nodded. At dinner, Troy had let her

in on a secret plan. Chad, Jason, and Troy were planning on meeting at the large rock by the bathrooms at midnight—for some late night pranks, no doubt.

"I'll be there. Don't worry," she whispered back to Troy. "I just hope no coyotes join us!"

Troy laughed and then raced after Chad and the others.

When Gabriella and Kelsi walked into their tent a few moments later, Taylor was already in her sleeping bag reading while Sharpay was lining up a series of plastic bottles and small containers.

Taylor, Kelsi, and Gabriella all stared at Sharpay in disbelief.

"A nighttime regime is imperative for a healthy complexion," Sharpay explained to her tent mates.

"Um, Sharpay," Gabriella finally said. "You might want to cut back on some of those sweet-smelling products. It's really buggy out here at night. You'll attract lots of bugs with all those creams and cleansers."

"Being itchy is the worst!" Taylor complained as she pulled a pair of socks onto her hands to keep herself from scratching her itchy poison oak. And getting labeled "lost girl" isn't much better, she lamented to herself.

Oblivious, Sharpay went on with her cosmetic routine. She didn't want to listen to any advice that Gabriella was giving out. After all, Gabriella didn't have the perfect pores, she did—and that all came from her rigorous nighttime cleansing regimen, which she followed religiously. She was not about to let a silly school camping trip get in the way of her having the most beautiful skin at East High.

"Oh," Sharpay said, waving her hand in front of her face. "What do you all know about beauty and keeping your skin perfect?"

"I know that there are a ton of mosquitoes out tonight," Gabriella said firmly. She reached into her backpack, pulled out her bug repellent, and sprayed.

"I just hope tomorrow goes a little better than

today," Kelsi remarked when everyone was settled in for the night.

"I second that," Taylor said before she drifted off to sleep. It had to be. . . .

CHAPTER EIGHT

"*Grrrrrrrrrrrrrrrrrrrr.*"

"Gabriella?" Taylor whispered. She leaned over and poked her friend. Gabriella let out a groan, and her eyes fluttered open. "Did you hear that?"

"*Grrrrrrrrrrrrrrrrrrrr.*"

"You mean *that*?" Gabriella asked, bolting up in her sleeping bag.

Kelsi switched on her flashlight. "What is going on?" she asked as she moved the beam of light around the tent.

The three girls all stared at each other with wide eyes as the sound coming from outside their tent grew louder.

"*Grrrrrrrrrrrrrrrrrr.*"

"Could that be a b-b-bear?" Kelsi stuttered. She pulled her sleeping bag over her head.

"How is Sharpay sleeping through this?" Taylor wondered out loud as she pulled her sleeping bag up to her chin. She leaned over to have a closer look at Sharpay, who had an eye pillow securely on her face and was snoring soundly.

"She's wearing earplugs!" Gabriella exclaimed, giggling. Then she considered Sharpay. "But maybe she was smart. I wish I hadn't heard that bear outside our tent."

Just then there were some rustling sounds followed by a loud *thump*. Gabriella checked her watch and breathed a sigh of relief. It was almost midnight. It had to be the boys getting their meeting underway and not a bear lurking in the bushes.

"Seriously! What. Was. That?" Taylor asked, jumping out of her sleeping bag and leaping onto Gabriella's.

Gabriella gave Taylor a reassuring look. "I am willing to bet that it's not a bear." She giggled. "Most likely, it's a bunch of Wildcats."

Kelsi stood up and walked over to the zippered front flap. She leaned down and unzipped it quickly.

"What, are you crazy?" Taylor shouted at her. "Don't go out there! There's a hungry beast outside!"

Kelsi didn't listen and climbed out of the tent. Taylor sat there petrified while Gabriella tried to decide if she should bust the boys.

"We should check on her," Gabriella finally said. She got up, grabbed her flashlight, and lifted the front flap of the tent.

"Wait!" Taylor cried. She picked up a small, round tin from her suitcase and held it up like a weapon. "I'm going with you."

As Gabriella climbed out of the tent, she saw a

gruesome—or rather, *boysome*—sight. Standing there in the bushes, illuminated by Gabriella's flashlight beam, were a few members of the East High varsity basketball team. Kelsi was in front, her hands on her hips.

"I was right. No bears, just some crazy Wildcats," Gabriella called back to Taylor.

Kelsi shook her head. "Not your best play, guys," she said.

Gabriella smiled at Troy. "You really scared us," she teased.

"Sorry," Troy said. "But we thought it was all just part of the camping experience."

"Not really," Taylor said, joining them. She glared at Chad. "I bet this was all your idea."

Chad shrugged and attempted to look innocent. "Hey, I was just along for the ride. But I have a question for you, what were you going to do with that tin? Bang the bear's head?"

Narrowing her eyes, Taylor gave Chad a mean look. "No, I was going to give the bear some chocolate chip cookies as a distraction, wise guy."

"Cookies?" Jason piped up. "You have chocolate chip cookies?"

"Not for any of you," Taylor snapped. Then she headed back into the tent.

Gabriella shrugged. "Well, boys, I think Taylor's had enough excitement for the night." She looked over at Troy and smiled.

"Sorry about the scare." Troy said.

"That's okay," Gabriella replied. "I had a pretty good feeling it wasn't a bear coming to get us."

"But it could have been the chief's ghost with his one-eyed coyote!" Jason exclaimed, trying to scare his friends.

"Very funny," Gabriella said as she and Kelsi fell into step beside Troy. "I think that I have had enough ghost stories for the night."

The group walked over to a large boulder where the full moon was shining down on the rock like a spotlight.

Gabriella couldn't believe how low the moon

was in the nighttime sky. The light was amazing. "This is incredible," she said.

Troy reached over and put his arm around Gabriella. "Incredibly romantic," he whispered.

"Shhh," Kelsi said, standing up on the rock. "I see someone over there."

Following Kelsi's finger, Gabriella's eyes grew wide. "Um, that's a little too tall for even one of the Wildcat basketball players," she whispered. She reached over and grabbed Kelsi's hand. "Oh, my goodness!" Gabriella gasped as she climbed up on the rock.

Kelsi squinted her eyes, scanning the area. That shape did look a bit too tall and wide to be a teenage boy. Her heart pounded in her chest.

"Holy moly!" Chad cried. He was now standing on the rock, too. Despite his earlier bravado, the idea that a real live bear might be only feet away scared him—big-time.

"Shhh," Troy said, not moving. "We need to be very still."

The bear was far away, but they could still see the large animal. The grizzly came down on his four legs and walked around in a small circle, roaring.

"What's he doing?" whispered Jason.

"Shhh," Troy hushed him.

After a few more turns, the bear quietly retreated back into the woods.

"Whoa, that was close," Kelsi said, giving a huge sigh of relief.

"You can say that again," Troy said. He shook his head. He had to admit even he was scared. Turning to Gabriella, he asked, "Are you all right?"

"Yes," she replied. "But I'm glad that he's gone. Good thing that we spotted the bear before he saw us."

Jason rubbed his eyes. "That was a little too real for me."

Kelsi and Gabriella giggled and sat down on the rock. The moonlight was so bright that they didn't need flashlights to see each other. In the stillness of the night, the girls sat quietly for a moment in the peaceful setting. Soon, Jason and Troy joined them.

"I guess Taylor really didn't want to come?" Chad asked Gabriella. He was feeling a little bummed out that she wasn't there to enjoy the scene with him. He had really wanted her to come along.

Feeling badly for Chad, Gabriella shrugged. "She had a long day. She'll be better tomorrow, I'm sure."

"Oh, that's cool," Chad said, trying to act like he didn't really care. He sat down on the rock next to his buddies. But it was easy to tell that he was disappointed.

"Um, guys," Jason said. He had stood up on the rock and was looking out on the clearing. "Is that Ms. Darbus lying over there in the grass?"

"What?" Troy said. He jumped up, ready to spring into action.

The group followed Jason's finger as he pointed. And sure enough, there was Ms.

Darbus, wrapped in a red flannel bathrobe, lying in the grass.

"Maybe she's been sleepwalking," Kelsi offered.

"Or maybe she was attacked by the bear!" Jason exclaimed. "She's not moving."

"The bear was wandering around here for a while," Chad said.

"Oh, my!" Gabriella cried into her hands. "We have to do something—fast."

They all started to panic and began talking very loudly. Suddenly, Ms. Darbus sprang up from the ground, and all the Wildcats shouted in surprise.

"What is going on here?" Ms. Darbus cried when she saw her students.

Gabriella was so relieved to see that her teacher wasn't harmed that she raced up to her and gave her a hug. "Oh, Ms. Darbus, we thought that you'd been attacked by the bear!"

"Oh, don't be silly," Ms. Darbus said, waving her hands. "I know all about survival in the woods. When I came out of the bathroom, I saw the large creature. I reached back to my formal acting training, and I thought about when I played Juliet in the final act." She looked around at her students who all had blank expressions on their faces. "You know, when Juliet fakes her death?"

"So you were just acting?" Troy asked.

"Why, yes," Ms. Darbus said, quite pleased with herself. "I knew that if I lay still the bear would lose interest and wander away." She sighed, pulling the tie on her robe tighter. "I just didn't count on being so convincing that I would relax completely and fall asleep!"

Everyone laughed. Then Ms. Darbus looked at her watch. Her face grew serious as she noted the time. "But what are you all doing up and out here at this time of night?"

"We were going to the bathroom," Gabriella said, grabbing Kelsi's hand.

"Yeah," Troy said. "Us, too."

"Us three, actually," Jason said, acknowledging Chad and Troy.

"Well, you all better get back to your tents right away," Ms. Darbus said. "You shouldn't be wandering around here in the middle of the night."

"Right, of course," Troy said. "Good night, Ms. Darbus." Then he winked to Gabriella. "Good night, girls," he said.

"Good night," Gabriella replied as they began walking to their tents. When Ms. Darbus was back in her own tent, Gabriella whispered to Troy, "That was close."

"No kidding," Troy said. "I'll see you in the morning, okay?"

"Um, you better get back to your tent quickly," Gabriella answered, looking to her left. She pointed to a large shape moving toward them. "I think the bear is coming back!"

The boys looked over and saw the large shadow. Letting out rather girly shrieks, they took off. Kelsi and Gabriella shared a smile.

"That was just too easy, huh?" Kelsi said.

"Yeah," Gabriella said, smiling. "But that big

bush over there does kind of resemble a bear. If I hadn't have seen it in the daylight, I would have been a believer, too."

Still giggling, Gabriella and Kelsi crawled back into their tent, the boys' scared shrieks echoing through their heads.

CHAPTER NINE

"*Ahhhhhhhhhhhhhhhhhh!*"

Once again, Gabriella, Taylor, and Kelsi were rudely awakened from a peaceful sleep. Only this time, the morning sunlight, not moonlight, was streaming into the tent. Looking over, the girls caught sight of Sharpay sitting in the middle of the tent with a compact mirror in her hand, screaming.

"Look at my face!" Sharpay cried out. "I am a red, blotchy mess!"

Gabriella took a closer look at Sharpay. Her normally smooth, glowing skin was indeed covered in red bumps.

"Don't scratch, Sharpay!" Gabriella warned her. "It will make the bites worse."

"And you could get scars," Kelsi added as she looked at Sharpay.

"Bites? Scars?" Sharpay screamed. Her mouth fell open. "Oh, no! This can't be happening. I look awful!"

"Is everything okay in here?" Ms. Darbus poked her head in the tent. "What is all the screaming about?"

"Look at my face!" Sharpay wailed, rushing over to her teacher.

Ms. Darbus examined Sharpay's bitten-up face. "Oh, dear. You must be so uncomfortable. Let's take you to the first-aid station right away and see if we can get you some ointment for those bug bites."

Quickly pulling on some clothes, Sharpay followed Ms. Darbus out of the tent.

"Well, that sure was an interesting way to start the day. But speaking of itchy, how are you feeling, Taylor?" Gabriella asked when Sharpay had left.

"Better," Taylor replied. But when she looked down at her hands and felt her face, she was only slightly relieved. The poison oak made her feel silly for getting lost all over again.

Smiling, Gabriella held out Sharpay's mirror to Taylor. "Take a look, you aren't as blotchy, either."

"I'm happy about that, but I sort of sympathize with Sharpay. She really got bitten up last night," Taylor said as she dressed. "She should have listened to you."

"She was warned," Kelsi put in. "I bet she isn't so thrilled with her nighttime regimen now."

The girls laughed and finished getting ready for the day. Kelsi picked up her team clipboard and checked the list.

"We still need to find a lot of things," she said

as they walked out of the tent.

"Not to worry," Taylor said confidently. She was a true competitor; she wasn't the president of the Scholastic Decathlon team for nothing. She would make sure her team came out on top.

When they arrived at the picnic tables for breakfast, most of the Wildcats were already sitting at the tables eating.

"Morning, fellow captain!" Martha called, catching sight of Kelsi. Martha was standing near the end of the food line holding her green clipboard in hand. "How's it going?" she asked with a grin on her face.

Kelsi held up her blue clipboard. "We're doing great, thanks," she said.

"Good to hear," Martha replied as she moved along the line. Ahead of her were two of the green-team members, Timothy Martin and Nathan James. "Nothing like a good competition, right, teammates?" she said. The boys both nodded their heads. Then Martha turned back to the girls. "Did you hear that some of the guys saw a bear last night? *And* that they saved Ms. Darbus from being attacked?"

"Oh, really?" Gabriella said, trying not to laugh.

"Wow," Kelsi said, finding it hard to stifle her own giggle. "They must have been *so* brave."

When Martha moved away, Kelsi faced Taylor and Gabriella and smiled broadly. "I guess the big bush worked its charm last night," she said.

"Yeah, maybe those boys will think twice about scaring us again," Gabriella mused. Catching sight of Taylor's blank look, she filled her in on what had happened after Taylor went to sleep.

Taylor was still laughing as Kelsi looked down at her clipboard and noticed the remaining empty check boxes. "All joking aside, we have a huge list to get through, and Martha is taking this very seriously." She looked over to where Martha was sitting. "Martha's got Timothy and Nathan on her team. Those guys are the best students in Mr. Gold's class."

"Maybe. But you've got me and Gabriella," Taylor said. She winked at Kelsi. "Clearly, we are going to win!"

"Exactly! Don't worry, Kelsi," Gabriella added. "We'll make sure we find lots of things on the list today."

As the girls moved along the food line, Zeke called out to them from his table. He was sitting with Chad, Jason, and Troy. "How's Sharpay? I heard that she had to go to first aid early this morning."

"Oh, she'll be all right," Gabriella assured him. "Just a little itchy."

"Did she get poison oak, too?" Zeke was noticeably concerned.

"No," Taylor said. "She was just a major attraction for some mosquitoes last night."

"Poor, sweet thing," Zeke whispered, causing some of the guys to groan.

Chad was sitting next to Zeke. He looked over at Taylor and flashed her a big smile. "Hey, you look much better than yesterday!"

Taylor rolled her eyes. She knew that her face had welts and that she was still swollen. "Are you lying to me?" Why did Chad have to bring up yesterday in front of everyone? And what did he mean by "better"? Was he just being nice? Or did she really look all right? She definitely didn't feel confident, that was for sure.

Taken aback by her response, Chad stood up and stammered a bit. "I meant that you look even more beautiful today," he said with a smile.

Now Taylor really felt like Chad was lying to her, and she wanted nothing to do with it. She took her plate of food and stormed past his table. She sat down at another one and stuck her fork in her eggs without looking up.

Kelsi stared at Chad and shook her head. "When a fish keeps opening his mouth," she said, "sometimes he gets hooked into more trouble." Kelsi tipped her hat and walked over to sit down next to Taylor.

Giggling at Kelsi's advice, Gabriella took a seat across from Troy.

Before she could even say hello, Mr. Gold banged a spoon on a large pot to get everyone's attention. "Good morning!" he yelled. "It's a beautiful day, and we're going to do some water testing. We'll break up into the blue and green teams and head down to the lake for the morning."

"Go, green!" someone cheered.

Taylor stood up. "Go, blue!" she yelled, pumping her fist in the air.

Kelsi shot Taylor a thankful look.

Troy glanced over at Gabriella. So much for spending the whole day together, he thought. He flashed a smile at Gabriella, hoping the afternoon would be different. "We'll have free time after lunch," he told her. "Let's go for a walk or something then, okay?"

"Definitely," Gabriella said, grinning back at him. She took a deep breath and looked around at their surroundings. "This place is a thousand times bigger than the roof greenhouse at school."

Nodding his head, Troy winked at Gabriella. "And we don't have to worry about anyone else snagging our spot."

"Yeah," Gabriella agreed. "We can just hang out. It'll be perfect."

At the next table, Sharpay had sat down in time to overhear Troy and Gabriella's conversation. She was now wearing a wide-rimmed straw hat and large sunglasses to hide her bites. The combination made her look more like a movie star on Rodeo Drive than a student on a camping trip. Leaning close to Ashley, she whispered, "I am so over those two."

"I know," Ashley whined. "At least Gabriella isn't on our team."

"That will be a nice break," Sharpay mused. Then she got up and walked over to Troy. "Oh, Troy!" she called. "Why don't we work together on the water testing?" She gave Gabriella a smirk. "You know, go, green team!"

"I see you're feeling better," Gabriella said to Sharpay, not rising to the challenge.

"Yes, Ranger Mike gave me some cream to put on my bites," she said as she nestled her way in to sit down next to Troy.

Ashley walked over, and Gabriella took in the girl's white halter top and short pink shorts. Gabriella stifled a sigh. It would be great if her bug repellent would work on pests like Sharpay and Ashley and keep them away.

Pushing aside such thoughts, she instead concentrated on the fact that Kelsi, Taylor, and the rest of the blue team were counting on her to help. She had to remember that during free time, she'd be with Troy—alone.

"See you later, Troy," Gabriella said with a smile. Then, turning to Sharpay and Ashley, she added, "Go, blue team!"

Rangers Nicole, Jessica, and Lou were assigned to the blue team. They led the group down to the lakeshore, and once everyone was seated on the soft sand, they began to explain the testing that they'd all be doing.

"We regularly test the pH of the water to measure the impact of acid rain," Ranger Nicole said as she handed out the water-testing kits.

"Can anyone tell me what causes acid rain?" Ranger Lou asked.

Taylor's hand shot up. "Acid rain is caused by airborne pollutants that combine with the water in the natural rain," Taylor explained. "This comes back down to the earth as acid, harming the natural environment. The air pollutants usually come from auto pollution and power plants as far away as China."

"Yes," Ranger Lou said, giving Taylor a smile. "Luckily, our region's ecosystem has not been impacted as much as other places in the country due to the prevailing winds. But it is always a good idea to do preemptive testing."

Everyone took a kit and got ready to begin. Ryan checked out the materials carefully. "This is like what I do for our pool at home," he whispered to Taylor. "Sharpay doesn't tolerate too much chlorine. She likes me to test the water a few times a day before she goes in. She says the chlorine is bad for her hair."

Taylor laughed. "Yes, this is kind of like that. Hey," she said, turning to include Kelsi, "I was thinking that for extra credit we could check the water for the level of healthy algae." She leaned over so that no one else could hear her. "I actually brought a microscope with me." She blushed a little. "I got a travel-size one for my birthday last year. It's really powerful but compact enough to travel."

"I didn't know they made minimicroscopes," Ryan said.

Taylor nodded and pulled a test tube out of her pocket. "We just need to collect a sample of the water."

Kelsi quickly got into the idea. Normally, she wasn't a competitive person, but she really wanted her team to do well. And more than anything, she didn't want to disappoint anyone, especially Mr. Gold, since he had picked her as a captain.

For the rest of the morning, the students tested the water for pH and dissolved oxygen and nitrates in different locations. They recorded the information in notebooks and carefully took notes on the experiments. They made other observations of the water quality and the active ecosystem. As the students worked, the rangers told them about the different species of fish in the water and other microscopic life-forms that lived in the lake.

"So it's not just fish in there?" Ryan asked, looking at the water he had collected with a new sense of appreciation.

"You got it," Ranger Jessica said. "The fish are just one part of the ecosystem."

"It's kinda like the cast and chorus of a show," Ryan said, realization dawning.

Ranger Jessica laughed. "Yes, it is. And each role is important for maintaining the show."

"This is much cooler than sitting in class and reading a textbook!" Jason exclaimed. He lifted up his sunglasses to feel the sun on his face.

Gabriella laughed and hugged her knees to her chest. She was enjoying participating in the experiments and being out by the water, only she couldn't help but wonder what Troy was doing on the other side of the lake. She looked at her watch, hoping that they could all return to camp soon. She was looking forward to spending the afternoon with Troy.

Finally, the blue team finished taking notes and packed up their supplies. Ryan patted his pocket to assure Taylor that he had the water sample for later. The group all filed into a line and walked back to the campsite.

When both teams had returned, Zeke ran over to Sharpay.

"How are those bites?" he asked.

"Better, thanks," she said. "Ranger Mike said that I was a victim because I am so sweet. Wasn't that thoughtful of him to say? He is totally nice." She cocked her head to the right and smiled. Then she looked back at Zeke. "Isn't he just the best?"

"Sure," Zeke said. He hoped she would appreciate his gesture as much. Reaching into his pocket, he handed Sharpay a small plastic container. "I whipped up some cream and mixed in some herbs that I saw down by the water. I think this will help soothe all the itching."

"You made that for me?" Sharpay asked, her brown eyes opening wide. She reached out for the canister and opened the top. A crisp, clean fragrance wafted out. "Hmmm, this smells great." She rubbed a bit of the mixture on her face.

"Um, yeah," Zeke replied. "I didn't want you to be uncomfortable the whole day. I hope it helps a little."

"Thanks," Sharpay said. She reached out to touch Zeke's arm. "Listen, Zeke, I talked to Ranger Mike this morning about the trail ride tomorrow. I explained to him that you and I are experienced riders and wanted to ride on the more challenging trails. So get ready for the ride of your life!" She took the container and ran back to her tent.

As Zeke watched Sharpay run off, he knew that he was in a major jam. He had to find a way to tell Sharpay that not only was he *not* an experienced rider, he was actually *afraid* of horses! Just thinking about riding caused him to break out in a cold sweat. The question was, how—and when—was he going to tell her?

CHAPTER TEN

After lunch, as Mr. Gold had promised, there was free time until dinner. Although it was technically "free time," the guidelines were very strict; all Wildcats had to sign out with Ms. Darbus, letting her know exactly what they'd be doing. Most of the group were going down to the lake to kayak or just hang out by the water. Troy and Gabriella decided on a hike.

"You need to stay on the marked trail," Mr. Gold told them as he handed out a detailed map of the area. After Taylor and Ryan's adventure, everyone was required to keep a map with them at all times. "And be back by five o'clock."

"Please do be careful," Ms. Darbus said. "We don't want any more drama out there in the woods."

After assuring Ms. Darbus that they'd be fine, Troy and Gabriella made their escape. They walked along a path that snaked through the trees. Gabriella couldn't stop grinning.

"What are you smiling about?" Troy asked, grabbing her hand.

"Just being here," Gabriella answered. "Isn't this great? All the reading we did about ecosystems and the environment means so much more out here, don't you think?"

"Yeah," Troy teased. "The science stuff is the only reason I'm having fun. It has nothing to do with being here with you."

Gabriella gave him a playful shove. "How was your morning?" she asked.

"It was cool," Troy told her. "We did the water testing." Then he started grinning. "And then I watched Sharpay and Ashley try to outflirt each other with Ranger Mike." As he said the ranger's name he swooned and held his hands under his chin. "They are treating him like some kind of celebrity. It's so funny!"

Troy and Gabriella walked on. "Look at those pinecones," Troy said a moment later, pointing ahead.

"The tree's a Douglas fir," Gabriella said, looking up. "See how the pinecones hang down on the branches? And they fall off whole." She leaned over and picked one up off the ground. "This is on the scavenger list." She handed the cone to Troy. "Give it to Martha when we get back."

"And you should give one to Kelsi," Troy said, offering Gabriella another cone. "I wouldn't have known that was a Douglas fir pinecone if you didn't tell me, so you should get credit for your team, too."

Gabriella felt another smile spread across her

face. Troy was so honest and so sweet. She really was the luckiest girl at East High.

As they continued walking along the trail, Gabriella told him about Sharpay's nighttime bug-attracting regimen and Ms. Darbus's morning hiking outfit.

"Where did Ms. Darbus get that hat with the netting?" Troy asked when Gabriella described the teacher's headgear.

"I know!" Gabriella said, laughing. "It's straight out of an African safari."

"You know what? I bet you she got it from the prop room," Troy declared.

As Gabriella and Troy walked along giggling, something caught Gabriella's eye. She came to a sudden stop. Reaching over, she pulled Troy's hand, signaling him to stop walking as well. "Look over there," she whispered. "At the base of that split tree."

Troy followed Gabriella's finger to what appeared to be a fuzzy white mound in between two round stones.

"Whatever it is, I think it's breathing," Troy said, noticing the rise and fall of the mound of white. He slowly walked over and crouched down on his knees to get a better look.

"I think it's a baby owl!" Gabriella exclaimed. She had followed Troy and now stood peering over his shoulder. "Poor thing must have fallen from its nest."

Troy tilted his head back and scanned the expansive branches of the trees above them. "I can't see where it came from, can you?"

Gabriella didn't move her eyes. She couldn't look away from the little owl. "Its feathers are so white," she cooed. "He looks like a cotton ball."

Suddenly, the little owl shuddered and its head twitched. With a tiny squeak, it buried its beak under its wing.

"Do you think it's hurt?" Gabriella said, her voiced laced with worry. Noting that it hadn't tried to move since they found it, she knew it couldn't be feeling well. They needed to do something.

"We should go get some help," Troy said, echoing Gabriella's thoughts. "I'm sure one of the rangers will know exactly what to do. You stay here, and I'll run to the ranger station."

She sat down on the ground and waited while Troy sprinted away. As she watched the baby owl, she decided that she'd call him Puff, because he was like a white puff of cotton.

"Hey, Puff," she said. "Falling from the nest must have been pretty scary for you. Don't worry, we'll find your mom." Watching the little owl, Gabriella's heart went out to the tiny creature. It was in a strange place without its mother. Being so close to her own mother made Gabriella feel even sadder for the wounded owl. "You just want to go home to your mom, huh?"

Gabriella looked back at the trail and hoped that Troy would return soon with a ranger.

Meanwhile, down on the lake, there were some intense boat races going on. Zeke, Jason, and

Chad were all in kayaks, paddling as fast as they could toward a red buoy in the water. With a shout, Zeke pulled ahead and, a moment later, let out a howl of victory. In their kayaks, Jason and Chad shook their heads, but they were also smiling as they conceded that Zeke was the winner.

On the sandy beach at the edge of the lake, Sharpay and Ashley were lounging in folding lawn chairs, not paying attention to the activity in the water. They were too busy soaking up the sun.

Under the shade of a tree at the other side of the beach, Taylor and Kelsi sat hunched over a textbook. Looking up, Taylor's gaze fell on Sharpay and Ashley. "Check out the bathing beauties," she said to Kelsi.

"Too bad suntanning isn't part of the science curriculum," Kelsi joked. "They'd be head of the class if it were."

Laughing, Taylor nodded. But then she looked at the bunch of leaf samples in front of her and sighed. Taylor and Kelsi were supposed to be identifying them, but they all looked way too similar. "I wish Gabriella were here," Taylor said. "She knows all these plant names."

"I know," Kelsi replied. "But it is free time. She was looking forward to taking that walk with Troy."

At that moment, Ryan walked up to their blanket and plopped down next to the girls. "Listen, I don't know much about this water sampling, but I was thinking . . ." He held up a tube of water. "I know we have already checked for healthy algae, but what if we checked for the toxic algae that Mr. Gold talked about last week in class? That could earn us some more bonus points and help out the park."

Taylor and Kelsi looked at each other in surprise. Where had Ryan come up with that idea?

Ryan shrugged sheepishly. "You aren't the only ones who pay attention in class," he explained.

The two girls quickly agreed, and with a plan

in motion, the three of them made their way back to camp so that Taylor could get her travel microscope from her bag. She quickly set up the device in the center of the tent and got to work. Carefully, she dropped a sample of water on a slide and placed it under the microscope. She peered in and then stepped back to give Kelsi and Ryan a look. As her friends were viewing the sample, Taylor reached for a book in her backpack.

"Ryan, I think you're on to something," she said as she skimmed a page. "Look at these pictures. Our water sample looks similar, don't you think?" Taylor pointed to a picture in the book that was of a toxic algae sample.

"I think we have something that we should tell Mr. Gold and Ranger Lou about," Kelsi said.

"Go, team!" Ryan cheered.

Gabriella tapped her foot and checked her watch once again. What was taking Troy so long? Had he gotten lost like Taylor and Ryan? She shuddered and pushed that thought aside. Hopefully, he was fine and would be back with a ranger—soon.

"Gabriella!" Troy called, as if on cue. He was running up the trail with Ranger Jessica at his side. The ranger was holding a box with a mesh top that Gabriella had seen used for transporting animals.

"Hi," Ranger Jessica greeted her. "You and Troy did the right thing by coming to get me. We have to be very careful with baby owls. I'll have to have one of the people from the bird rehabilitation center take a look at the little guy."

"Do you think he's all right?" Gabriella asked.

"Well, if we're lucky, he's just shaken up and his mother will take him back into the nest," Ranger Jessica said as she covered her hands with gloves and carefully put the owl in the box. "Lucky for him you spotted him here."

But Gabriella wasn't listening to the last part of what Ranger Jessica said—she was stuck on one thing. "His mother might not take him back?" Gabriella asked, horrified. That seemed so cruel and unfair.

"Hopefully, there hasn't been a lot of time since his fall and she will," the ranger said. "But, yes, sometimes wild animals will turn their backs on their young—if they smell humans, for example."

"Poor Puff." Gabriella sighed.

"You named him?" Troy asked.

When Gabriella shrugged, Troy grinned. He shouldn't have been surprised. It was just like her to be so sweet and name the animal.

Ranger Jessica closed the lid of the box carefully and looked over at Gabriella. "I promise that as soon as I hear any news I will come and find you both. You did a great job here. Thank you."

The ranger turned to go back down the path, but paused. Looking over her shoulder she warned Troy and Gabriella not to say anything to their friends—not yet. The fewer people who knew, the better. The students, thinking they were helping, could come to see the owl and only make the situation worse. They might even disturb the nest.

Troy and Gabriella quickly agreed even though they knew it would be hard. Then, saying goodbye, they headed back to camp, their thoughts full of hope for little Puff.

"Man, Troy should have been here," Chad said as he pulled his kayak up on the shore. "That race was awesome."

"No. That race was a workout," Jason complained, rubbing his arms. Then he smiled. "But totally fun. Zeke, you were great out there. You sure know how to maneuver a kayak."

"Thanks," Zeke said. He wished that Sharpay had noticed his victory out on the water, but she had been engrossed in a magazine the entire time.

Since Zeke was on dinner duty for that evening, he said good-bye and headed back to camp. Jason and Chad took their time walking and ran into Sharpay and Ashley.

"Have you boys seen Troy?" Ashley asked. "He was supposed to help us find some birds for our scavenger-hunt list."

Chad shrugged. "He and Gabriella went for a walk."

"Figures," Ashley sniped. "Where is Troy's sense of teamwork?"

"What do you mean?" Jason asked, annoyed that she might be saying something mean about one of his guys.

Ashley shifted the lounge chair that she was carrying and flipped her hair over her shoulder. "I'm just saying that those two are not on the same team and spent the whole afternoon together. It would have been nice if they helped their teams look for things like birds."

"Oh, Ashley, those two don't need to look. They are birds—lovebirds," Sharpay said with a moan.

"Well, they'd better not be swapping information," Ashley huffed. "I, for one, need some extra-credit points for Mr. Gold's class."

"Me, too," Sharpay said, an image of a new car flashing through her mind. Suddenly, her eyes narrowed.

"Oh, look," she said, pointing. "Here they come now."

Up on a hill, Sharpay spotted Troy and Gabriella holding hands as they walked. When they saw their friends, Troy and Gabriella waved but didn't immediately join them. First, they went to speak to Ranger Lou. Shaking their heads, Sharpay and Ashley left to freshen up.

"What was that all about?" Chad asked Troy when the pair finally came and sat down under the tree where the others were sitting.

"Gabriella and I had to talk to Ranger Lou," Troy said, shrugging.

Before Troy had a chance to go on, Jason jumped in.

"Sharpay and Ashley are all over you guys for not being team players," Jason told them. "They are all steamed up about you taking off."

Gabriella tried not to make a face. "Let me

guess, they have the green-team spirit?" she asked, thinking that those girls were just green with envy, not team pride.

Chad chuckled at her joke. "You could say that."

Glancing over at the picnic tables where a group of students were congregating, Gabriella snapped back into focus. Her hand flew to her mouth. "Oh, I am on dinner duty tonight. I have to run," she said as she took off.

"See you!" Troy called. He shook his head. Even a walk during their free time had proved to be exciting and full of drama. With Gabriella, there was never a dull moment.

CHAPTER ELEVEN

Gabriella and Zeke stood next to each other as they chopped vegetables for the chili the group was having for dinner. Parked near the picnic tables was a large white truck that functioned as a giant refrigerator. And alongside the truck was the makeshift kitchen with folding tables where the Wildcats could prepare the food.

"Zeke!" Ranger Mike called from the fire pit that was off to the side. "I heard that you are a master baker. Any ideas for a special dessert tonight?"

Smiling, Zeke nodded to Ranger Mike. "For a bonfire night? That's easy. There's nothing more perfect around a campfire than a s'more," he said. "Toasted marshmallows melting a piece of chocolate on crunchy graham cracker. Delicious!"

"Yum!" Gabriella exclaimed. "Can we have those?"

"I think we can arrange that," Ranger Mike replied. He lifted a large pot onto the grate lying over the fire.

"You know they're called that because you just can't have *one*," Zeke told Gabriella. "You always want *some more*!"

Gabriella chuckled and reached for another carrot to chop. "Very clever," she said. "I'm up for skipping the chili altogether and just eating dessert right now!" Changing the topic, Gabriella lowered her voice and leaned in to whisper to Zeke.

"Have you talked to Sharpay about the ride yet?" she asked. She stopped dicing her carrot to look Zeke in the eye. She was genuinely concerned about his well-being.

Avoiding Gabriella's stare by scooping up his carrot pieces, Zeke dumped them in the bowl before he answered. "No," he mumbled, "I haven't found the right time."

Shaking her head, Gabriella put a hand on her friend's shoulder. Looking around to make sure no one could overhear, she went on. "Zeke, you have to tell her that you are afraid of riding. Ranger Mike told us that there are jumps on the trail and that the experienced riders gallop most of the way. You *can't* go on that trail if you don't know how to ride."

Zeke held back a groan. Gabriella was right. Tomorrow was the trail ride, and he was running out of time. He'd have to find a way to tell Sharpay before he got himself in serious hot water.

At the next table, Ryan was opening cans of black beans to pour into the pots. He had heard every word of Zeke and Gabriella's conversation and knew that he had to tell Sharpay. She might be interested to know just how far Zeke was willing to go to impress her.

"Good work, Ryan," Ranger Mike said, giving him a tap on the back. "Could you open these cans also?" He pointed to a case of beans. "Thanks, you're a good sport."

When Ranger Mike's back was turned, Ryan shot him a glare. His hand was starting to hurt from the manual can opener. He was having fun, but he missed the idea of electric appliances in the kitchen and of others cooking for him. With a sigh, he picked up another can. He'd have to tell Sharpay about Zeke's secret later.

Away from the cooking, Taylor and Kelsi were doing some more research on toxic algae in water. Since discovering similarities between their water sample and the example in the book, they were convinced they were on to something big. But they wanted to know what they were talking about when they met with Ranger Lou.

They had set up a nice place to read under a tree near their tent.

"Hey, there," Martha said when she spotted them. She walked closer and leaned over to see what Taylor and Kelsi were reading. "What are you doing?"

Taylor pulled the book up to her chest. "Oh, just catching up on some stuff," she said.

"Yeah," Kelsi agreed. "You know, enjoying the great outdoors."

"I see," Martha said, her eyes narrowing suspiciously. Those two were up to something—she was sure of it. "You guys should really keep your eyes up instead of in a book if you want to catch the green team."

Taylor scowled at Martha. Normally, she loved Martha's competitive nature. When they were at a Scholastic Decathlon event, she could always count on Martha to come through with the right answer in a clutch. But now, with Martha as the competition, it wasn't quite as much fun.

"Oh, I would worry about catching up with *our* team," Taylor taunted. "We've got a lot of answers already."

"Well, we'll see about that," Martha said before heading off toward the picnic tables.

Kelsi checked her clipboard and frowned. "Taylor, we actually don't have a lot of the answers. I'm not sure we're going to win."

"Stop thinking that we're not going to win," Taylor chastised. Then her mouth turned up into a gleeful smile. "We'll totally get extra points for this algae finding."

"Not to mention," Kelsi added, "saving a few fishes' lives."

With determined nods, the girls went back to their research.

Taylor and Kelsi were silent as they focused on their project. But their peace and quiet was interrupted by Chad. He was still trying to get back in Taylor's good graces and hadn't seen her much until now. Jumping up on a rock behind them, he shouted, "Hello, ladies!"

His sudden—and rather loud—appearance startled Taylor, and she dropped her book. "Chad, you made me lose my place!" Taylor fumed. Gathering up her papers and book, she quickly headed back to her tent without another word.

Chad stood frozen. He was totally losing his touch out here in the wild. Every time he tried to get near Taylor, she ran away like *he* was poison oak.

Without a word, Kelsi picked up the blanket and ducked in the tent after Taylor.

"Gee," Chad said with a sigh. "Those two are supertouchy!"

He looked around to see if anyone had witnessed Taylor's major blow-off. Man, he thought, I've got to get my game back soon. I need some new offense—and fast.

The five-alarm chili that Ranger Mike and the group of Wildcats made for dinner was a big hit. But that didn't stop everyone from eating quickly. They wanted to head down to the lakeside for the bonfire.

"If everyone would please take their dishes over to the wash bins," Mr. Gold announced, "we can start down to the beach for the evening activity."

Everyone cheered and brought their plates over to the large tubs filled with soapy water. Standing behind the tubs, looking very unhappy, were Ashley and Sharpay. Much to their disappointment they had been assigned cleanup duty that night.

Ryan was one of the first ones done with his dinner. Heading to the tubs, he handed his dirty dish to his sister and tried not to smirk. She was all decked out in designer waders, looking like she had stepped off the pages of their father's fly-fishing catalog.

"Oh, you don't have to be so glib," Sharpay accused Ryan.

"I didn't say a thing!" Ryan cried, raising his hands up innocently. He was greatly amused to see his sister work cleanup dressed in waders and rubber gloves. "But, quick question—did you catch any of those elusive plate fish yet?"

"Just move along," Sharpay huffed, ignoring her brother's bad joke.

"Hold on," Ryan said. He wanted to tell her about the conversation that he had overheard between Zeke and Gabriella. "I have a serious question—"

"Oh, come on, Ryan," Sharpay snapped. "Move it!" She gave him a cold stare.

"Fine," Ryan said. "If you are *so* busy, then I won't tell you."

"Tell me what?" Sharpay asked.

The line to drop off dirty dishes was growing, and people were starting to yell for Ryan to move out of the way.

"Oh, nothing," Ryan said as he turned to walk off. "I guess you'll find out soon enough."

"Yuck!" Sharpay cried as more students dunked their plates into the soapy water, carelessly splashing her with chili remnants.

As Gabriella handed over her plate, she noticed Sharpay's rather odd outfit choice.

"You thought to bring rubber gloves and waders for cleanup duty?" Gabriella asked. Leave it to Sharpay, she added silently. That girl was a walking, talking fashion show.

"Well, of course," Sharpay responded. "I am not about to ruin my manicure or shoes because of a camping trip. Now, could you wash that plate yourself?"

Gabriella was about to answer, but just at that moment Ranger Mike walked over with a fresh tub of water. As soon as Sharpay and Ashley caught sight of him, they stood up straighter.

"Good job, girls," the ranger said as he placed the new water on the ground. "You'll be done in no time and then we can all get over to the bonfire."

Sharpay and Ashley nodded at Ranger Mike's command. Then Sharpay reached out to take Gabriella's dirty plate.

Stifling a giggle, Gabriella held her hand to

her mouth. Ranger Mike was having a nice effect on Sharpay and Ashley.

Still laughing to herself, Gabriella strolled over to Troy. Together they followed the rest of the Wildcats down to the lake and found seats close enough to the fire to stay warm, but not in the way of the smoke.

Gabriella looked up at the dark sky. The stars were hidden behind the clouds, making the night extradark. She shivered and moved closer to Troy.

"Have you seen Ranger Jessica?" Troy asked.

"No," Gabriella whispered back.

As she spoke, Troy put his arm around her shoulders and Gabriella felt her heart skip a beat. "Did you see Sharpay and Ashley doing the dishes?" he asked, changing the subject.

"That was a sight," Gabriella agreed.

"Watching Sharpay do cleanup was totally worth a trip out here!" Troy said with a laugh. "But it has definitely not been the best part." He gave Gabriella's shoulder a squeeze.

As all their friends gathered around, Troy and Gabriella continued to huddle together. Zeke walked around the circle handing out graham crackers, chocolate bars, and marshmallows. Jason and Chad both pointed their flashlights at Zeke so that he was illuminated as if he were a rock star on a stage. When everyone had their ingredients, Zeke demonstrated the fine art of crafting the perfect s'more.

"Get me s'more of that!" Chad yelped after Zeke passed him the finished sample.

Troy and Gabriella waited on line to roast their marshmallows and then sat back down to layer up the treat the way Zeke had showed them.

Kelsi watched Gabriella and Troy laughing and eating their gooey treats. "Don't get me wrong, I'm happy their having fun," she said, turning to Taylor. "But I feel like we haven't spent any time with Gabriella today at all."

"I know, it's strange," Taylor said. "Gabriella doesn't even know about our algae finding."

Before they could go on, the night filled with sounds of music. Max Rosen, one of the kids in the school band, had brought his guitar and had begun strumming. Gabriella took the cue and began singing. At first, Troy was shy and didn't sing very loudly. But by the time the chorus came along, he was belting out the words with his favorite singing partner.

"Another duet," Sharpay mumbled as she and Ashley walked up to the bonfire, their cleaning duty done.

"Sticky sweet," Ashley said in agreement after following her friend's gaze.

"Speaking of sweet," Sharpay said, shifting the lounge chair she was carrying to her other shoulder. "I see a perfect spot over there."

Ashley followed Sharpay as they both squeezed their way through the crowd and sat down.

As soon as she was comfortable, Sharpay started singing along with the guitar music, eager to show off her talents. Her bug bites had subsided and she seemed in a better mood.

"Hey, Sharpay!" Zeke called out. "I made a special s'more for you. Extra chocolate."

Glancing up behind her, Sharpay noticed Zeke holding a s'more out on a red heart napkin.

She stopped singing. "Thanks," she said, reaching for the sweet treat.

Zeke smiled and quickly walked back to his seat. He hoped that his dessert would make Sharpay happy.

As Max began to play another campfire favorite, Troy saw Ranger Jessica walking down the path and nudged Gabriella. He raised his hand and waved, but it was too dark for the ranger to see them.

Trying to get the ranger's attention, Troy and Gabriella stood up. Unaware of what was going on, Chad and Jason stood up, too.

"Hey, where are you going?" Chad asked.

"Are you ditching already?" Jason added.

"Oh, no," Troy said. "We just need to talk to Ranger Jessica."

"Oh, right," Jason said with a mischievous grin. "We get it. Time with your lady." He turned to trade a high five with Chad.

Chad nodded, then he looked seriously at Troy. "But you didn't have to lie. We get it."

Troy felt his face grow red. If only he could tell them what was going on. But they had promised the ranger. "No, no," he said, instead. "It's not like that."

Before he could say more, Gabriella grabbed Troy's hand and they raced around the circle to get to the ranger.

"Is there news?" Gabriella blurted out when they reached her.

Even though it was very dark, Gabriella was able to see Ranger Jessica's mouth curve into a smile. That had to be a good sign.

"Puff's all right," the ranger said. "He does not appear to be hurt from the fall."

Gabriella started to jump up and down,

but the ranger put her hand up.

"Well, hold on," she said. "First we have to locate his nest, and we're not sure how long he was out of it. There's still a chance that the mother won't take him back. If that's the case, we'll have to send him to the bird-rehabilitation center."

Gabriella gasped. "Poor Puff!"

"But," Ranger Jessica continued, "we don't think that is the case. We think you found him in time."

"Thank goodness!" Gabriella exclaimed. She glanced over at Troy and saw that he looked as happy as she felt. It was a good thing they had taken that walk.

Troy squeezed Gabriella's hand. "So what happens now?"

"It's too dark tonight, so early tomorrow morning we need to find the tree with the owl's nest. The bird rehabilitation crew will carefully place Puff back, and we'll see how it goes." Ranger Jessica looked at Gabriella and Troy in the dim light. "Do you think that you can remember the exact spot where you found Puff?"

"I think so," Troy said.

"We'll have to," Gabriella assured the ranger.

There was a huge cheer from the crowd as Max began playing a popular song that everyone knew.

"Why don't you go back and join your friends, and we'll meet at the rangers' station before breakfast," Ranger Jessica told them.

"Before breakfast?" Troy asked. "Man, that's gonna be early."

Gabriella gave Troy a shove. "We'll be there," she said. "We'll definitely be there."

CHAPTER TWELVE

Gabriella was wide awake when her tiny alarm clock beeped the next morning. She had been so nervous about oversleeping that she had barely slept at all. She quickly turned off the alarm and jumped out of her sleeping bag. She couldn't wait to see Puff again. She just hoped that she and Troy would be able to remember the exact spot where they had found the little owl and get him home.

"I know the answer," Taylor mumbled, causing Gabriella to startle.

148

For a moment, Gabriella stood frozen, waiting to see if Taylor would wake up. Taylor must be talking in her sleep, she thought when her friend didn't open her eyes. Gabriella didn't want to have to lie about where she was going so early in the morning. But Ranger Jessica had told them that the fewer people who knew, the better. So Gabriella's plan was to leave a note that she had gone for a run and would meet her friends at breakfast.

"A high level of nitrates in water results in a decrease of oxygen," Taylor said as she flopped over and snuggled deeper into her sleeping bag.

Whew, Gabriella thought, that was close! Quickly, she looked to make sure the other girls weren't awake. Kelsi was sound asleep, curled up and hugging her pillow. And Sharpay, with her large, purple spalike eye mask on her face, was snoring in a steady rhythm. Silently, Gabriella got dressed and then slowly unzipped the tent flap and crawled outside. As she zipped the door back up, she paused, hearing Taylor rolling around again. With a fast tug, she pulled the zipper the rest of the way and scooted over to Troy's tent. She hoped that he had remembered to set his watch alarm.

Troy's alarm *had* gone off, but his arm was tucked under his pillow so he didn't hear it for a few minutes. Finally, the dull beeping woke him up. His tent mates were all sound asleep, but he still tried to be extraquiet as he pulled on his clothes. Just as he was about to slip out, Chad's head popped up from across the tent.

"Where are you going?" Chad asked, rubbing his eyes. He raised his wrist and tried to focus on the numbers on his watch. "It's way too early to get up."

"Shhh," Troy said, trying to keep his voice low. "Go back to sleep." He thought quickly of something to say. "I'm just going out for a run."

Chad shot him a look. "Now? The sun isn't even up."

Troy shrugged. "You know what my dad says, it's never too early to be in training."

"Well, hold on," Chad said. "I'll come with you. I could use a run. Plus, I need to talk to you about Taylor. She seems really mad at me. I'm not sure what to do."

Troy glanced at his watch. He was late. He had to move faster. "No!" he said quickly. Then he realized he had said that too harshly. "I mean, you should get your rest. I'm just going to run alone."

Even as he was talking, Troy knew he should stop and just get out of there. Gabriella was probably already waiting for him. And if they were going to show the ranger where they found Puff and do it before breakfast, he had to move fast. He grabbed his sneakers and slipped them on.

"But we always run together," Chad started to mumble.

Troy, however, didn't hear him. He was already out of the tent. Chad lifted up the window cover near his bed and peered outside. He saw Troy running across the campsite—and right next to him was Gabriella.

So much for wanting to run alone, Chad thought as he punched up his pillow and threw his head back down. All this fresh air is really making people act all wacky.

As soon as they had said good morning, Troy and Gabriella ran to the ranger station. Troy felt a pang of guilt as they sprinted. He hated blowing off Chad. His buddy seemed upset about Taylor, which was suprising. They had been getting along—or so Troy thought. He'd have to make sure to find Chad later and hear him out. He wondered if Taylor had said anything to Gabriella. But before he could ask her, they reached the station. Ranger Jessica was waiting for them on the porch.

"Right on time," Ranger Jessica said with a cup of steaming coffee in her hand. "Thanks for making this early-morning effort."

"How is Puff doing?" Gabriella asked. "Is he all right?"

"Yes," Ranger Jessica assured her. "Puff is doing great. Come with me, and I'll show you."

She led Gabriella and Troy to a room in the back of the station. On a table under a window was a small box. Peering inside, Gabriella and Troy saw Puff, sleeping peacefully.

Gabriella sighed. "He looks so sweet," she said.

"And pretty comfortable," Troy added.

"The little guy is doing okay. But the best thing for him right now is being with his mom," the ranger told them.

"I've been thinking about it all night, and I'm pretty sure I know exactly where we found Puff," Gabriella said.

Troy nodded. "It should be an easy walk from here," he added.

"Perfect," Ranger Jessica replied. She made her way back to the front room. "The folks from the bird-rehabilitation center aren't here yet, but we should head out to the trail anyway."

Gabriella and Troy followed the ranger out of

the small wooden cabin. As they walked along, Gabriella pointed out things that they had seen on their walk—and then she saw the split tree and two stones.

"Look, Troy!" she cried out. "I think this is it! This has to be where we found Puff."

Troy looked around. "I think you're right," he said. "This is definitely the tree."

Ranger Jessica took her binoculars out of her pocket and aimed them up toward the branches. "Hmm," she said. "That might be a nest way up there." She pointed to the right side of the tree. Looking back at Troy and Gabriella, she smiled. "This has been a huge help. But now you both need to head back to camp for breakfast. Once the bird specialists arrive, I'll come find you with news."

"Can't we stay until the rehabilitation people get here?" Gabriella pleaded. She couldn't stand not knowing if Puff would be an orphan.

"I think it's better if you go back," Ranger Jessica told her. "I promise I'll find you as soon as there is any information. And now that we have found the nest, you are free to share your story with your friends. I'm sure they'd love to hear it."

Saying good-bye, Troy and Gabriella walked back to the campsite.

"Puff is going to be fine," Troy said, grabbing Gabriella's hand.

"I hope so," Gabriella replied. She squeezed his hand. But even Troy's reassuring grip did nothing to ease the nervous feeling in her stomach.

At the picnic tables, the topic of the day seemed to be Gabriella and Troy's early morning "run." Contrary to what Troy thought, *everyone* had noticed their sneaking off.

"He totally blew me off," Chad complained to Zeke and Jason as he stabbed his fork into a stack of pancakes.

"The bigger question should be what you were doing up before the sun?" Jason teased. "You're more of the night owl type."

Chad gave Jason a look. "I'm just saying those two have been spending a lot of time together." Dragging a piece of pancake through a puddle of syrup, Chad sighed. "There are other people who need to talk to Troy," he added.

Noting Chad's grumbling, Martha leaned over from her spot at the next table. "They better not be sharing any team information," she said. "Right now the score is pretty even."

"Gabriella wouldn't do that," Kelsi said as she walked by Martha's table and overheard the other leader's comment.

"And no way is Troy a cheater," Jason said, jumping in to defend his friend.

"I'm not saying that they *are* cheating," Martha clarified. She stood up with her empty plate. "But I'm watching them." She turned and took her plate over to the bucket of soapy water.

As if on cue, Sharpay's voice rang out. "Oh, look!" the drama queen called from the food line. She lifted her finger and pointed across the way. "Here come our resident lovebirds."

Everyone turned to watch as Troy and Gabriella walked across the center of the camp-site.

"So much for making a quiet entrance," Troy leaned down and whispered in Gabriella's ear.

"I guess people did notice that we were gone," Gabriella replied. She gave a small wave to Kelsi and Taylor. When the two girls didn't return it, Gabriella gave Troy a confused look. What was going on? she wondered.

"Hi," Gabriella said tentatively when she reached her friends' table.

"Where have you been?" Taylor asked. She pulled on Gabriella's hand to make her sit down at the table. Before Gabriella could respond, Taylor went on. "People are starting to talk about you and Troy sharing information for the scavenger hunt. The competition is getting pret-ty intense." Taylor looked over at Troy, who was standing with Chad. She shot them both a stern look. "And it doesn't help that you are *always* with Troy."

"What?" Gabriella cried. How could people accuse her and Troy of cheating? "No way."

"We didn't think so," Kelsi said, reassuring her friend. "But we thought you should know."

"I got you some breakfast," Troy said, appearing at the table with two plates of steaming pancakes.

"Thanks," Gabriella said, trying to sound friendly as she took one of the plates. But her friends' words were ringing in her ears.

"We could really use your help later, Gabriella," Taylor said as she stood up. "Come on, Kelsi. We have to go meet Ranger Lou at the staff table." Taylor looked at Troy. "Official blue-team business."

"We'll see you at the team meeting after breakfast, right?" Kelsi asked Gabriella, looking meaningfully at her friend.

"Of course," Gabriella answered. How could she think that I wouldn't be there? Gabriella wondered sadly.

Once Taylor and Kelsi were gone, Gabriella leaned over to Troy. "People are really taking this scavenger hunt seriously. They didn't even give me a chance to explain where we were. I was going to tell them all about Puff."

"I know," Troy said. "The guys were the same way with me. Chad nearly bit my head off when I tried to talk to him."

Gabriella sighed and looked over at the staff table where Taylor and Kelsi were now seated. Ryan was there as well. "I wonder what that is all about," Gabriella said.

Troy looked over at the unlikely trio. "Official blue-team business, I'm sure," he joked. "Come on, let's eat these pancakes before they get cold."

Gabriella took a bite, but she found she had no appetite. She took a deep breath, wishing that Puff would be okay—and that her friends would give her a chance to explain her side of the story.

CHAPTER THIRTEEN

Ranger Lou scanned the paper that Taylor had handed him. He took a long, slow sip from his extralarge coffee mug and looked up at the three students sitting across from him.

"Which one of you brought a microscope on a camping trip?" he asked.

"A real scientist always needs to be prepared," Taylor boasted.

"Of course," Ranger Lou said with a smile.

He turned to Mr. Gold. "You have some pretty dedicated students here."

"Yes, indeed," Mr. Gold said, grinning.

"So, what do you think, Ranger Lou?" Ryan asked, leaning forward. "Is there toxic algae in the lake?"

"Well, there is always some level of toxic algae in the water," the ranger said.

"Are the fish in danger?" Taylor jumped in.

"Let's hope not," the ranger responded. "All kinds of algae are part of the balance of the ecosystem. But we always need to check, and we'll certainly follow up on your findings."

"So we might have discovered something useful?" Ryan asked.

"The information from this area of the lake is always changing," Ranger Lou told them. "And it is good to be kept up-to-date. The earlier we have indications of a problem, the better."

Taylor nodded at Kelsi and Ryan.

"Great work," Mr. Gold said. "I'm proud of you for taking the time to collect the data. And that you remembered what I said in class about toxic algae."

Ryan winked at Taylor as he straightened the purple cap on his head.

"I am going to send a sample out to the lab this morning, and I'll get back to you about their findings," Ranger Lou said.

Kelsi held up her blue clipboard. "Go, blue!" she cried.

"That went well," Ryan said as they walked over to join the rest of their team.

"Good thing that you brought your microscope," Kelsi added.

Taylor smiled again. "I knew it would come in handy."

"Come on," Ryan said, picking up the pace. "The rest of the team is waiting for you, Kelsi."

Kelsi looked at the group of students and felt a little overwhelmed. Being the captain was hard! Especially when it meant she had to talk in front of all those people. Sighing, she made her way over. But her team wasn't the only one gathering.

"Green team, we are a machine," Martha rapped. "We're the number one team!"

As the green team echoed Martha's cheer, Martha waved to Kelsi . "Hey, Kelsi!" she called. "Are you guys ready for the green machine? Because we're ready for you!"

The green team let out cheers of appreciation and a few members—including Sharpay and Ashley—even busted out dance moves.

Sharpay and Ashley pulled Troy up front to dance with them. Everyone was getting into the green-team spirit.

Panicked, Kelsi looked at her team. Even though she had written a whole musical by herself, she felt overwhelmed by the idea of inspiring her team the way Martha had. She hung her head. How could she be a leader if she couldn't even lead?

"Go ahead," Taylor said, encouraging Kelsi to get the meeting started.

"You can do this," Gabriella mouthed to her. "Go ahead."

Kelsi turned back to face the crowd. "Hello, blue team," she said softly.

"Louder!" someone cried from the crowd. "Speak up!"

Taking a deep breath, Kelsi yelled, "Hello, blue team!"

"Blue team rocks!" Jason called, pumping his fist in the air.

"Rock it to the top!" Kelsi shouted, feeding off the vibe of the group.

The team responded with a chorus of "Blue rocks, blue rocks, blue rocks!"

The group's enthusiasm gave Kelsi the energy and confidence that she needed. She took another deep breath. She hushed the group. It was time to get down to some serious business.

"There are a lot more items left to identify on our list," Kelsi said. She glanced around the group. Everyone was listening, their attention completely on her. "We only have a few hours this morning, so let's keep our eyes open and check those items off!"

"Go, blue team!" someone cheered.

Kelsi grinned. Maybe she wasn't such a bad captain, after all.

With her pep talk over, the blue team dispersed. It was time for that morning's activities. The students had a choice of exploring the trails, the water, or the skies for animal life.

"Sharpay," Zeke said, walking up behind her. "What group are you going with?"

Sharpay kept her eyes glued on the group of rangers over to the left. She was trying to listen to the chatter among them to figure out which group Ranger Mike would be leading.

"I was hoping that we could be in the same group," Zeke went on, unaware of Sharpay's plan. Please say yes, he wanted to add. He was thinking that now was a good opportunity to come clean about his fear of horses. He shifted his feet in the dirt, and then looked up at Sharpay, waiting.

"Sure, whatever," Sharpay said absently, still trying to figure out what Ranger Mike was saying. She was slowly inching her way over to the circle of rangers.

Zeke sighed in relief. Yes! This was his chance! "So about the trail ride tonight," he started to say, but just then the rangers started to break off.

Ranger Mike held up his hand. "All birdwatchers, follow me!" he yelled.

Before Zeke could finish his sentence, Sharpay was off—leaping and pushing her way over to Ranger Mike's side.

"All right, then," Ranger Mike said, looking a bit confused by the sudden interest in birdwatching. "Let's head this way and keep our eyes open for some amazing birds," he announced and led his group up the trail.

Zeke's shoulders sagged. "Um, so I'll see you later, I guess!" he called after Sharpay.

This was not good, he thought. The ride was tonight. In a few short hours, Sharpay would find out that he was not just a bad rider but that he was a liar, too.

Zeke wasn't the only one striking out. Chad

was not having much luck with Taylor, either. He had tried to talk to her all morning, but she kept avoiding him. Finally, as the students broke off into their groups, he saw an opening. Taylor was alone—and not scowling.

"Hey, Taylor!" Chad called.

Taylor turned to see Chad running over to her.

"How are you feeling today?" he asked, somewhat tentatively. He had no desire to make Taylor mad again or to be on the receiving end of one of her angry glares.

"I feel great, thanks," she said coldly.

"The poison oak looks under control," Chad said, looking at her face. He gave her one of his most charming smiles.

But Taylor wasn't paying attention. She was trying to find the group heading down to the lake. When she spotted Ranger Nicole on the lake path, she turned to Chad. "Listen, I have to run. See ya."

"Wait, um, I'll go with you," Chad said.

But Taylor was already gone.

Chad stood still, feeling as if the opposing team had just grabbed the basketball right out of his hands.

"Um, okay," he said. He felt a little funny standing all by himself in the center of camp. "I'll see you later!" he called after her, trying to save face. He didn't want everyone to know that all his efforts with Taylor were failing.

But they were—big-time. He shook his head and tried to psych himself back into his groove.

Kelsi was also planning to head down to the lake, but first she wanted to show Gabriella the two kinds of plants that were still on the blue team's list. Kelsi was standing with Gabriella and pointing to her clipboard, but she soon realized that Gabriella's eyes were not on the paper.

"Are you listening?" Kelsi asked, looking up at her friend. "Gabriella!" she shouted, waving her hand in front of her friend's face.

Gabriella's brown eyes snapped back into focus. The early-morning meeting with Ranger

Jessica had tired her out more than she realized.

"I'm sorry, what were you saying?" Gabriella asked when she saw Kelsi staring at her.

Kelsi shook her head. She had had enough. "I didn't want to believe what Sharpay and Ashley were saying about you and Troy, but Gabriella, you've been very distracted. I'm not sure if you are giving information to Troy and the green team, but I know you haven't really been a part of *this* team."

Gabriella felt as though she'd been slapped. She valued Kelsi's opinion and hated to think the other girl was doubting her. She tried to regain her composure so she could speak.

But Kelsi took Gabriella's pause to mean that she didn't care. Exasperated, Kelsi walked off and joined the other blue-team members in the group heading to the lake trails. Other people were counting on her. She was the captain. She couldn't let them down—even if Gabriella was letting *her* down.

"Kelsi! Wait!" Gabriella called. But it was too

late. Kelsi was already gone. Gabriella kicked a rock across the path in front of her. She'd have to do some fast talking next time she saw Kelsi. This was more than not just being a good team player—suddenly Gabriella didn't feel like a good friend.

CHAPTER FOURTEEN

After the morning activities had been completed, the groups returned to camp for lunch. Taking advantage of the free time before the meal was served, Ryan went and found Sharpay. He'd been meaning to talk to her about Zeke. He found her sitting alone at a picnic table.

"What are you doing?" Ryan asked. He was surprised to see Sharpay without an audience of some kind.

"Ranger Mike asked for some volunteers to

171

help out with lunch," she told him. She looked around at the empty area. "I'm a little early," she admitted. Then she leaned in close to whisper in Ryan's ear. "Promise me you won't let anyone at home know about this cooking stuff. Promise!"

Ryan smirked. "Oh, your secret is safe with me," he assured her. Until he needed dirt . . .

"Did you know that Ranger Mike used to ride in a cavalry?" Sharpay asked. Following his sister's gaze, Ryan saw the ranger setting up the fire pit. "He isn't just a ranger, he's a cowboy!" she added.

"Wow," Ryan said. He sat down on the bench next to his sister. "So he rides horses, too."

Sharpay touched her head to make sure her ponytail was still straight. "Isn't that just perfect?" she said with a giddy laugh. "And he is so knowledgeable about birds. Did you know that male and female birds have different color feathers? It helps with mating."

"Fascinating," Ryan said, trying to keep a straight face.

"He told me all about it so I could write up a little report for Mr. Gold." Checking to see if her nail polish had chipped, she stared at her hands. "Extra credit."

"Extra time with Ranger Good Looking is more like it," Ryan said with a smirk.

"Hmm, maybe," Sharpay mused with a far-off look in her eyes. Then she snapped back into focus, turning to face her brother. "Did you need something?"

"That's going to be some trail ride later—for everyone," Ryan hedged.

"And you know what?" Sharpay squealed, not catching the leading tone in her brother's voice. "Zeke told me he rides, too. We're going to go on the expert trail. How great is that? It is so much better to have another rider who can keep up."

"Uh-huh," Ryan replied. He took off his cap and ran a hand through his blond hair. "You know, I heard something I thought you should know."

Sharpay turned and looked into Ryan's eyes. "Ooh, what is it?" she asked. She was always interested in hearing gossip, especially when it was juicy.

"All I know is someone might end up with their face covered in mud later on," Ryan said mysteriously.

Sharpay's brown eyes twinkled. "Oh, tell me who!" she exclaimed. "Is it Gabriella and Troy?"

"No, it's not them," Ryan said, shaking his head.

"How about Ashley?" she asked. She rolled her eyes. "She's really been crowding my space lately."

"No, not Ashley," he said.

Sharpay looked stumped. "Then who?"

Ryan paused. He wanted Sharpay to take this seriously. Zeke was a good guy, and he was just trying to impress Sharpay. If anyone should be the one calling out the lie, it should be Zeke himself. Ryan looked down at his very dirty shoes. He rubbed a smudge on his right foot. "You know what, it's something a bit more personal," he finally said.

But as Ryan lifted his eyes, he saw that his act of kindness didn't matter. Sharpay wasn't even paying attention. Ranger Mike was opening up the truck to unload the food for lunch.

"I'll have to catch you later, Ryan," Sharpay said as she jumped off the bench and headed over to help Ranger Mike. "You can tell me then!"

"Okay!" Ryan called after her. He put his cap back on his head and stood up. What could he do? She was going to find out sooner or later— whether he told her or not.

"Hey, Ryan!" Taylor shouted, interrupting his thoughts.

Ryan turned to see Taylor, Kelsi, and Ranger Lou walking toward him.

"We got the official water tests back," Ranger Lou said. "It seems that you two stumbled upon some valuable information."

Taylor was grinning, and Kelsi looked like a proud team captain.

"That really *was* toxic algae?" Ryan asked. He knew that they had studied the pictures in the book closely, but it was still shocking.

"Yes, we've already taken the necessary steps to help rebalance the water," Ranger Lou said. "We could have had a serious problem on our hands if not for you guys."

Taylor threw her arms around Ryan and gave him a hug. "Good job," she said.

"Wow," Ryan said. "I can't believe we actually helped."

Ranger Lou laughed. "Well, you did. We rangers owe you many thanks, Wildcats."

As soon as Ranger Lou walked away, Kelsi traded high fives with Taylor and Ryan. "Great job!" she cried.

"Thanks!" Taylor exclaimed, grinning. "But I wouldn't have been able to do it without Ryan."

Ryan tipped his cap. "The pleasure was all mine!"

"Well, now that that is taken care of," Kelsi

said, "can someone please help me record a warbling vireo?"

"Is that a snake?" Ryan asked, slightly alarmed.

Taylor and Kelsi laughed and grabbed Ryan's hands as they walked toward the wooded trail.

"No, it's a bird!" Kelsi told him.

Ryan stopped midstep. "If you remember, last time Taylor and I went stalking an animal, we got into some trouble." He looked over at Taylor and winked.

Kelsi pulled him forward. "No worries. We won't leave the area. There should be some vireos around here somewhere."

"Hmm, how about I get some lunch and see if one flies over for a bite?" Ryan said, rubbing his empty belly. But from the look on his teammates' faces, he knew that wasn't going to be an option. "Didn't think so," he said.

A grin spread across his face. He pulled something out of his pocket. "I do happen to have a minirecorder, courtesy of the drama department."

While lunch was being made, Troy and Gabriella slipped off to see how Puff was doing.

"You are worrying too much," Troy said to Gabriella as she expressed her fear for Puff yet again. Still, as they ran up the path to the rangers' station, he took Gabriella's hand and gave it a reassuring squeeze. Reaching the building, they walked up the steps and knocked on the door.

"Hello!" greeted Ranger Jessica. "Please, come in."

"Do you have any news?" Gabriella asked, getting right to the point.

Ranger Jessica smiled. "Yes," she said. "All went well with the reunion."

Gabriella and Troy let out a cheer.

"We'll have to keep a check on him, but so far so good. Great work," the ranger said, congratulating them.

With the good news fresh in their minds, Gabriella and Troy went back to camp. "I'm glad everything worked out," she said as they walked, "but I wish finding him hadn't made everyone so mad. Even Kelsi is upset. And I can't really blame her." She looked into Troy's eyes. "We haven't really been there for our friends."

Troy picked up a small branch on the trail and threw it. "I know," he said. "And it doesn't help that everyone is so stressed out about this scavenger hunt."

"It was supposed to be fun," Gabriella agreed.

"Well, this afternoon's trail ride to the new campsite will give us a change of scenery," Troy pointed out. "Maybe that will help."

"Let's hope," Gabriella said. But then she let out a gasp. "Poor Zeke! He still hasn't told Sharpay the truth, has he?"

"I don't think so," Troy replied, feeling bad for his friend. "One thing I do know, he better do it before we hit the trails."

* * *

By the time Troy and Gabriella made it back to camp, lunch was ready.

"Please line up to the left for grub!" Ranger Mike shouted to the hungry Wildcats. "We've got hot dogs and burgers for everyone!"

"Excellent," Jason said to Chad as they moved into the line. "All this exploring and experimenting is making me hungry."

"Dude, you are always hungry," Chad said with a grin. Then he scanned the crowd for Taylor. It was time to find out what the deal was with her.

He spotted her standing with Kelsi and Ryan by the edge of one of the trails. He ran over, resisting the urge to scream out her name. Instead, he played it cool and gently tapped her on the back.

"Hey, Taylor!" he said, trying to sound free and easy.

"No!" Taylor cried. She turned to see Chad standing behind her. She narrowed her eyes.

"We've been waiting to catch a warbling vireo singing so we could record the sound, and now you just scared it away!"

Chad was speechless. Once again, his timing was all wrong. He thumped his fingers on his leg. "Uh, sorry," he said. "I just wanted to tell you that lunch is ready."

"Lunch?" Ryan exclaimed. "I am so there!" He waved and ran toward the food.

"All right, fine," Taylor said, a bit dejected. She huffed off behind Ryan.

Once again, Kelsi found herself alone with Chad. She noticed the hurt look on his face as Taylor walked away. "I know you are trying to be nice to Taylor," she said gently, "but she's just a little edgy since she and Ryan got lost. You have to understand that."

"Edgy is putting it mildly," Chad said. Then he leaned in closer to Kelsi and whispered in her ear, "So it's not me? She's not just mad at me?"

Kelsi put her hand on Chad's shoulder. His

curly hair was springing out from under his red Wildcats cap. "Chad, did it ever occur to you that she might just be mad at herself?"

Chad stared at Kelsi for a minute. Her question threw him off his game. "What do you mean?" he asked.

Kelsi sighed. "Did you ever consider that Taylor might be really embarrassed about getting lost? And that maybe, just maybe, she hates that you know she got lost? You checking in on her all the time only serves to remind her." She started to walk toward the food line.

"Huh," Chad replied, taking in what Kelsi had said. That wasn't his intention. He had just been trying to look out for her. But maybe he had been *trying* too hard. "I guess I have been in her face," he said, catching up with Kelsi. "I just didn't know what else to do."

"I know," Kelsi said. "Ease up on her a bit. She'll come around in time."

Chad nodded. Kelsi was giving him some good pointers. He would lay off and see what happened. Maybe this afternoon's horseback ride would be a good way to make up—and give him a fresh angle.

"Thanks, Kelsi," Chad said. He clapped his hands and got psyched for the afternoon. Everything would work out. It had to.

CHAPTER FIFTEEN

"Do you need any help taking down your tent?" Gabriella teased Troy as they finished lunch. Everyone was getting ready to pack up so they could move their campsite. The trail ride would take them to another area of the park where they would have their night-sky lesson. "I'm not sure you can handle it. As I recall, you had some problems setting up."

"Very funny," Troy said. "I think the boys and I can handle the taking down."

At that moment, Jason came up and sat down. "Dude, you've *got* to talk to Zeke," he said. "I think he is really serious about going through with this expert trail ride."

"That would be a total shock," Troy replied. "I guess he wants to play this out, but I think he'll change his tune once he sees the horses up close and personal."

Jason nodded. He knew that Zeke had a crush on Sharpay, but he wondered how far it would take him.

As the three friends walked back to their tents to pack up their things, Gabriella spotted Sharpay. "Get a load of that," Gabriella said, pointing up ahead.

"Wow," Troy said as he noticed Sharpay's outfit. "You gotta hand it to Sharpay. She certainly knows how to dress the part."

Sharpay was wearing beige jodhpurs with dark leather patches on the inseams. Her brown-and-black-striped top fit her perfectly, and the matching velvet riding hat on her head was the same chocolate brown color as the leather patches. She looked like she was ready for a hunt in the country rather than a trail ride at a state park, but she clearly didn't care.

Glancing down at her old jeans, Gabriella sighed. "I can't believe I'm saying this, but now I feel underdressed for a horseback ride."

Meanwhile, Sharpay soaked in all the attention that played up her role as horseback-rider *extraordinaire*.

Zeke was among the onlookers. "You look great," he said, coming up beside her. He rubbed his hands on his pants, trying to stop them from sweating. Just seeing Sharpay in the riding outfit made his stomach do some major flipping and flopping. There was no way that he was going to be able to get up on a horse.

"Oh, this old outfit?" Sharpay said to Zeke. "Please, it's just necessity. Every rider knows that, right?" She winked one of her brown eyes at him. "Didn't you bring your own helmet?" she asked.

"Um, no," Zeke managed to say. He took

a deep breath. "Listen, Sharpay, I . . ."

Before Zeke could finish his sentence, Martha came running over. "Quick! Green-team meeting, guys!" she yelled. "Over by the picnic tables."

Sharpay shrugged and followed Martha to the meeting spot, leaving Zeke still trying to find the words—and the courage—to tell Sharpay the truth.

Kelsi looked down at the blue box that had all her team's findings from the past few days. There were samples of various plants and written pages of observations that needed to be checked against the list fastened to her clipboard. Kelsi just hoped they had enough to beat the green team. Mr. Gold had instructed them to hand in everything before the ride.

Seeing Kelsi alone, Gabriella saw an opportunity to apologize to her friend. She went over to where Kelsi was standing. "I'm really sorry, Kelsi," she said. "I know that I've been a little distracted and probably not the best blue team member." Gabriella took a deep breath, hoping Kelsi could see just how badly she felt.

Peering over her glasses, Kelsi gave Gabriella an inquisitive look. But she didn't cut her friend off. Instead, she waited to see what Gabriella had to say.

"Troy and I . . . well, we . . ." Gabriella started to stutter. "We had another project that we were working on," she finally said. "It was not green or blue related." Then Gabriella smiled. "Actually, it was white. See, we found a baby owl that had fallen out of its nest. We had to wait to find out if the mother would take him back, but everything seems to have gone well." Gabriella stopped for a moment. "Except now everyone is mad at me and Troy."

Kelsi pushed her glasses up onto her nose and smiled. She couldn't stay mad at Gabriella: she had saved a baby owl. Kelsi's grin grew sly. "Well, I guess I can forgive you, if . . . the owl is all right now?"

"Yes," Gabriella said, knowing that Kelsi's

teasing smile meant she understood why she had been so preoccupied. "He's back in his nest with his mom."

"That's great!" Kelsi exclaimed. "Well, seeing as that project is taken care of . . ." She looked down at the team box. ". . . can you help me get this ready for judging?" she asked.

Gabriella let out a huge sigh of relief. All was well.

Together the two girls organized all the blue team's samples, drawings, and observations. When they were done, Gabriella went to pack up the tent, and Kelsi took the box over to Mr. Gold.

"So how are we doing, Captain Blue?" Ryan asked, tapping her on the shoulder as she walked past.

"Good," Kelsi said, smiling.

"Blue rocks!" Ryan cheered. He pulled his duffel bag onto his shoulder and hauled it over to the truck, which was going to meet the students at the new campground.

Kelsi watched Ryan walk off, and then continued over to the table where Ranger Lou and Mr. Gold were sitting. She put her team's box down.

"Everything completed?" Mr. Gold asked.

"I think so," Kelsi replied.

"Good job, Kelsi," Mr. Gold said with a smile.

Kelsi nodded, hoping that her team box had more items in it than the green-team box Martha was holding.

"Hello, Kelsi," Martha said as she placed her box on the table.

Kelsi gave a wave.

"You were both terrific captains," Mr. Gold said, taking a quick peek into both boxes. "We'll announce the winner at the final bonfire tonight."

As Kelsi walked away, she couldn't help but feel a bit unsure. It wasn't only her grade on the line, her whole team was counting on her.

"Hey, what's wrong?" Taylor asked Kelsi when she saw her by the luggage truck. "I know you are the captain of the blue team, but that's no reason to look so blue!" Taylor laughed at her own silly joke.

Kelsi smiled at Taylor's attempt to make her feel better. Choosing not to admit her worries, Kelsi replied, "Oh, I was just missing my music, especially my piano. I've really never been away from my music for so long."

"I understand," Taylor said, putting her arm around Kelsi's shoulders. "But you're doing a great job here. The blue team is *rockin'*!"

"But can we rock past the green machine?" Kelsi asked. "It's going to be tough waiting until tonight to find out the winner."

Taylor nodded. "Yeah, but I can't wait to see the look on Martha's face when we win!"

Just then, Ranger Mike clapped his hands. "Everyone ready to ride?" he asked. He was trying to round up the students to head over to the stables where the horses were waiting. "We need to get moving!"

Kelsi looked over and noticed that while everyone was following the ranger, Zeke was slowly backing away. "Hey, Zeke," she said. "Um, you okay?"

Feeling a little self-conscious, Zeke looked at Kelsi and Taylor carefully. "The guys told you about basketball camp, didn't they?"

"Um, no," Kelsi said. "It's just that you look like you are about to skydive off a cliff, not go for a little horseback ride."

Zeke shook his head. That was exactly how he was feeling. He quickly filled Kelsi and Taylor in on his situation. "Listen, please don't say anything to Sharpay," Zeke pleaded when he had finished. "I'm sure that I'll be fine once I get on the horse." He paused for a moment. "I hope."

Just then, Troy and Chad came up behind Zeke, catching the last part of his conversation. Troy slapped him on the shoulder. "Zeke, she's going to be able to tell right away."

"Like when you pass out!" Chad chuckled.

With his head down, Zeke followed the other students to the stables. When he saw the large horses sticking their heads out of the stalls, waiting for their riders, his heart began to race—and not in a good way.

Sharpay had gotten there early to survey her horse options. After a few moments, she settled on a tall black gelding named Beau. She stroked his nose and gave him a carrot piece from her pocket. "Good boy," she cooed. Then she turned to see Zeke standing at the entrance of the stable. "Hey, there!" she called to him.

"Hay is for horses," Zeke replied, trying to make a joke.

Sharpay smiled. "Maybe you want to ride Walnut? He looks like a beauty." She motioned toward the stall next to Beau's.

Zeke peered in and saw Walnut standing in his stall. He was the largest horse Zeke had ever seen. He gulped.

Down the aisle, Chad was trying to get Taylor's attention, but she once again was avoiding him. Chad took a proactive move and slid up to her in line.

"I'd like to ride with you," he said.

"You mean you want to keep tabs on me?" Taylor said, glaring at him. She put her hands on her hips. "You think I'm going to get lost again? Is that why?"

Chad took a step back. "No, I . . ." he started to say.

"Look, I'll see you later," Taylor snapped, and she moved ahead down the aisle to pick her horse.

"Wait, Taylor!" Chad called. He reached out to grab her arm. "I just . . ."

"You just what?" Taylor asked, turning to face him.

Chad took a deep breath and decided to take an honest, straightforward pass. He looked right into her eyes. "I just miss hanging out with you. I never meant to make you feel worse. Every time I asked if you were okay, it was because I just wanted to see you—pure and simple."

A smile slowly spread across Taylor's face. "Really?" she gushed. "That's it? That's the *only* reason?"

Chad nodded his head and smiled.

"Come on, cowboy," she said, the iciness gone from her demeanor.

Chad gave a Texas cowboy holler. "Let's hit the trail!"

Still frozen in front of Walnut's stall, Zeke saw Chad and Taylor take two horses out of their stalls and join the lineup. Taking a deep breath, he grabbed Sharpay's arm.

"Sharpay, I have to tell you something. I'm *not* an expert rider," he blurted out. "I'm not even a rider. In fact, I'm really afraid of horses."

"You're afraid of horses?" Sharpay asked. For about a minute, she didn't blink.

Zeke shook his head. "I know I shouldn't have lied to you. It's just that you were so excited about riding. And I really wanted to be on the trail with you."

"You could have been seriously hurt," Sharpay scolded when she finally spoke.

"I guess it wasn't just my ego that would have been bruised, that's for sure," Zeke said with a laugh. "The last time I was on a horse, I fell off."

Sharpay's expression softened. "You should have been honest with me."

"I know," Zeke said. He hung his head and turned to walk away. He had blown it. Keeping his eyes on his feet, he wished his sneakers were on the glossy wood floor of the gym where he was always so comfortable.

Sharpay watched Zeke's slumped shoulders as he walked away. "You know what they say!" Sharpay called to Zeke's back.

Zeke turned around. "What's that?"

"Once you fall off a horse, you have to get right back on." Sharpay gave him one of her super center-stage smiles. "Not only am I an excellent rider, I happen to be a good teacher, too."

Ranger Mike was outside the far end of the stable. He looked comfortable seated on his carmel-colored mare. "All my expert riders!" he called.

"We're leaving for the ride now. All the beginners, please follow Ranger Nicole over on the left."

"Are you sure?" Zeke asked when Sharpay made no move to follow Ranger Mike. It was her big chance to go riding off into the sunset. "You'd ride with me?"

"Of course. Riding is riding. Plus, I never got to thank you for that face cream you made me. Now, first," Sharpay said, "let's get you up on a horse." She grabbed Zeke's arm and led him over to a stall away from Walnut.

Outside, Troy was pulling himself into the saddle. He was riding a mare named Annabel. When he was settled with his feet in the stirrups, he pointed to the paddock outside the stables. "Look at that," he said.

Gabriella followed Troy's finger and couldn't believe her eyes. "Zeke is on a horse!" she cried. She pulled back gently on the reins to stop her mount so she could take in the scene.

Sharpay, on Beau, was leading Zeke on a small gray horse that was stepping very slowly. As they

197

walked, Sharpay talked to Zeke and corrected the position of his hands on the reins.

"The dude is totally doing it!" Chad cheered as he watched his teammate.

Zeke would have waved to his friends, but he didn't dare take his hands off the reins. Instead, he looked up and smiled. He wasn't center court or in front of an oven, but Zeke had to admit to himself that he was feeling good. Grinning at Sharpay, he exclaimed, "I'm riding a horse!"

"Yes, you are," Sharpay said, unable to resist his enthusiasm.

"You can go ahead and hit the expert trail," Zeke said. "I'll understand."

"It's all right," Sharpay said. "It's not a big deal."

Zeke beamed. He knew that this was not only a big deal for him but for Sharpay, too. "I can't believe that I am saying this," Zeke said as he smiled at Sharpay, "but *giddyup, horsey!*"

CHAPTER SIXTEEN

The trail wrapped around the mountain. Since they started the ride late in the afternoon, the sun was now setting, throwing beautiful light across the sky. The Wildcats were all enjoying the scenic ride that would take them to the other side of the park and the new campsite.

From atop her horse, Kelsi looked at her friends. She smiled when she saw Chad and Taylor riding side by side on the trail behind her. When she caught Chad's eye, she winked. She was glad that he had listened to her advice and that he and Taylor had worked things out. They both seemed really happy.

And they were. "Wow, this is incredible," Taylor was saying. She looked off to her left at the brilliant colors streaking across the sky. "The view is unbelievable. When Ryan and I were in the woods, we could only see part of the sky." She paused and took a look at the wide, expansive view. "But here, the sunset is just amazing."

"I know," Chad agreed. "It is amazing." But as he said it, his eyes were on Taylor, not the sky.

Taylor blushed and quickly tried to change the subject. "You look like you know what you're doing on that horse," she told Chad.

Now it was Chad's turn to turn red. "I have ridden a few times before."

"Well, I am glad that you are riding with me now," Taylor said, giving Chad a warm smile.

For the first time since Taylor and Ryan had gotten lost, Chad was feeling back in a groove with Taylor. She wasn't mad at him, and they were having fun. "Yeah," he said. "This nature stuff is okay with me."

"Kelsi!" Ranger Nicole called out from the front of the line.

Busy looking around, Kelsi jumped when the ranger yelled her name.

"Don't let Butterscotch eat the weeds on the side of the trail," Ranger Nicole advised. "Keep her head up!"

Kelsi struggled with the reins, trying to gently encourage her horse to move forward. But Butterscotch seemed determined to chew the tall grass that was so close to her nose.

"Um, she doesn't seem to want to stop!" Kelsi yelled up to the ranger.

Butterscotch flipped her mane and brought her head up.

"Oh, you don't like me talking about you, huh?" Kelsi said to the horse. She gave Butterscotch a loving pet. "Well, let's get this straight," she said, leaning toward the horse's ear. "You take me down to the campsite, and I'll get you a little snack when we get there. How's that?"

Her horse seemed to like the idea and moved on down the trail. Kelsi was feeling pretty proud of herself. She sat a bit taller in the saddle as she guided Butterscotch down the trail.

But Kelsi wasn't the only one having trouble. Troy's horse, Annabel, was also snacking on shrubs instead of following the horse in front of her.

"Easy, girl," he said, pulling the reins. "How about a little more walking and a little less snacking, huh? We need to catch up with everyone."

Gabriella looked over her shoulder and giggled. "She's not listening. It looks like you're not much of a horse whisperer."

Sighing, Troy gave Annabel a gentle pat and then a slight nudge with his heel. "Come on, girl, we can do this. See how Pal is walking with Gabriella?"

Just at that moment, Troy heard the sound of

rapid hoofbeats coming up behind him and Gabriella.

"Oh, my!" Ms. Darbus called out as she flew past her students. "Look out ahead!"

Troy pulled on his reins as hard as he could. Annabel moved to the side of the trail, just as Ms. Darbus rode by on her horse, Cocoa. It seemed the teacher's horse wanted to lead the pack, not follow. Ms. Darbus was just along for the ride.

"Whoa!" called out Ranger Lou, who was overseeing the middle of the group. In one quick motion, he reached out and grabbed Cocoa's reins. The horse stopped with a loud neigh.

When her horse was steadied, Ms. Darbus let out a dramatic sigh. She looked gratefully at the kind ranger. "Oh, thank you," she said, a hand to her heart. "And I thought controlling a classroom of teenagers was difficult!"

Ranger Lou smiled over at Ms. Darbus. "No trouble," he said, tipping his hat gallantly. "No trouble at all."

"Wow," Gabriella whispered to Troy. "That

was kind of romantic how Ranger Lou saved Ms. Darbus."

"You need to hold tight and don't let Cocoa get the lead," Ranger Lou added, continuing to coach their teacher.

"You can do it, Ms. Darbus!" Ryan cheered. He was riding along on a spotted brown horse who, unlike the others, was giving him no trouble. "Just *act* like a rider and the horse will respond."

"Good advice," Ranger Lou chimed in. "Horses can sense if you are unsure and will take full advantage."

Ms. Darbus laughed. "Just like a classroom of teenagers!"

The excitement over, the chain of horses continued to follow the lead horse along the winding mountain trail. While Kelsi's and Troy's horses occasionally still tried to eat shrubs, the other riders got the hang of it and kept moving the horses along. Ms. Darbus was even able to control Cocoa, and she started settling in to enjoy the sunset ride. For a while, the group fell silent as they took in the sights. The only sound was the steady clip-clop of hoofbeats and the occasional snort.

Soon, the new campsite came into view. It was in a valley, surrounded by low hills. In the center, there was a wide-open space with a bonfire already set up.

The Wildcats rode their horses over to a line of stakes in the ground. Two rangers greeted them and helped them get off the horses. Everyone was a bit sad that the ride had come to an end, even Zeke.

"That was better than I imagined," Zeke said. "Sharpay, thank you."

Sharpay blushed, uncharacteristically. She swung her leg over and jumped off her horse. Then she looked up at Zeke in the saddle. "You're a natural," she said. Turning back to her horse, she removed Beau's bridle and slipped on his halter. When he was secured to the stake, she began to brush him.

"Just be prepared to be a little sore tonight,"

Ryan warned Zeke as he walked by.

Zeke nodded, understanding. His muscles were already starting to protest. "That's cool," he said. "I wouldn't have traded that ride for anything."

When all the horses were brushed and cooled off, and munching on hay and oats, the Wildcats gathered around the bonfire.

"We hope that all of you had a nice ride out here," Mr. Gold said to the group. "We're getting dinner ready and then we'll have our final bonfire and Ms. Darbus will lead the storytelling. Not to mention the announcement of the winner of the scavenger hunt," he added.

"What about the tents?" Nathan asked. He was looking around for the supplies.

Mr. Gold smiled. "Yes, well, we decided that for a special treat we'd all sleep under the stars tonight."

A huge cheer erupted from the group.

Holding up his hands for quiet, Mr. Gold got everyone's attention. "Clearly, there will be some ground rules, so please listen carefully. First, I need all of you on dinner duty to report to the food truck. The rest of you, please stay around here, and we'll let you know when it's time to eat."

"But what about all the bears?" Ami asked. She was standing with some of the other cheerleaders who didn't look too happy about sleeping without a tent. "We heard a few people saw bears the other night."

"No worries," Ranger Mike assured them. "No bears around here."

Ami sighed and looked over at Ranger Mike thankfully.

Troy looked over at Gabriella. "Let's go talk to Ranger Jessica. Maybe she has an update on Puff."

They both ran over to the ranger who was busy pulling boxes of food out of the supply truck.

"Hi!" she greeted Gabriella and Troy as they raced up to her. "There hasn't been one peep or hoot from the nest," Ranger Jessica told them. "All is well."

Gabriella squealed in delight.

"If you hadn't found him when you did," Ranger Jessica continued, "and acted so quickly, the little one would have had a hard time. Thank you for being such keen observers and for helping out."

"What's going on?" Ashley asked, appearing beside the supply truck. If something was up, she wanted to know about it.

"Well, your classmates just saved a baby owl from being orphaned," Ranger Jessica told her. "And tonight they'll be honored for their good work."

Gabriella looked over at Troy and smiled.

"Honored?" Ashley said. The surprised look on her face quickly turned to one of jealousy. "Is anyone else going to be honored?"

"Actually, yes," the ranger replied. "I believe that we have a whole award ceremony planned for you all after dinner."

Hearing that, Ashley smiled. She loved attention—and awards.

For once, Ashley's spotlight-hogging didn't bother Gabriella. She was too happy about Puff to be concerned with Ashley. Gabriella looked over at Troy. "I am going to find Kelsi and Taylor and fill them in."

Troy nodded. He had to tell the guys, too. And then get ready for a perfect, star-filled evening.

CHAPTER SEVENTEEN

The sun was well below the horizon as the Wildcats gathered around a roaring bonfire in a wide circle. Ranger Lou walked around in the middle of the circle, holding the talking stick. He shot a wink at Ms. Darbus and then began to speak. "We are happy to introduce you to a traditional Native American dance troop," Ranger Lou said to the East High students. "They will dance and chant an homage to Mother Earth. After they finish, we will begin our story circle, and the passing of the talking stick."

"Cool," Chad said, already getting into the beat of the drummer sitting on a rock by the bonfire. He carefully watched the dancers around the fire. "Check out those moves!"

The six male dancers were dressed in authentic Native American clothes with headdresses and feathers in their hair. Their dance was full of spirit and emotion. Everyone was taken in by their energy and focus. At the end of the performance, all the Wildcats stood and applauded.

"We'd love to invite you all to come up and dance with us," the man who was playing the drum said. He motioned for people to get up and dance with the troop.

Sharpay was the first to jump up, with Ryan at her side. Sharpay and Ryan never missed an opportunity to dance. They looked like they were having so much fun, that soon everyone, from the basketball team to the Scholastic Decathlon team, was up and moving around the fire.

"That guy has awesome moves," Martha

remarked. She was loving the beat and did her best to keep up with the fast rhythm of the drum.

Not to be left out, Ashley joined and was soon out of breath as she struggled to keep up. "This is harder than any exercise DVD I own!"

When the drums finally stopped, everyone returned to their seats. Ranger Lou raised the talking stick to get everyone's attention. The other rangers, Mr. Gold, and Ms. Darbus helped quiet the crowd.

Ranger Lou then handed the stick to Ms. Darbus. "I just want to explain a little about this stick," she told the Wildcats. She pointed to the top of it. "This is an eagle feather and it is tied here at the top of the stick. The feather gives the holder the courage and wisdom to speak truthfully and wisely. And the rabbit fur on the end of the stick reminds the speaker that words must come from the heart and that they must be soft and warm."

"Wow," Kelsi whispered. "That is really cool."

"Are you going to take a turn?" Gabriella asked from the seat beside her.

"I do better with musical notes than words," Kelsi said. "And since there's no piano here, I think that I am going to pass. But you and Troy should tell the story of how you found the owl."

Gabriella's eyes grew wide. She turned to Troy. "What do you think? Should we speak next?"

"Sure," Troy said, noticing how eager Gabriella was to tell the baby owl's story. "It will be a good way to let everyone know we weren't intentionally ditching them!"

Martha was the first to go. Ms. Darbus handed the talking stick to her and everyone got very quiet. After Martha finished her story about the first rap song she ever heard and how it had changed her life, Gabriella raised her hand. Ms. Darbus handed her the stick. Gabriella stood up with Troy at her side.

"We were walking down the path in woods," Gabriella began. She told the story of how they found the baby owl. Then Gabriella gave the stick to Troy, and he told the group how the ranger called the specialists in to help put the owl back in the nest.

As Troy was speaking, Gabriella saw Ranger Jessica beaming with pride. Even Sharpay looked impressed. When they were finished, everyone applauded, and hooted, of course.

"Three hoots for you! Hoot! Hoot! Hoot!" Chad yelled, pumping his fist in the air. He slapped Troy on the back. "So that's why you were sneaking off, huh?"

Troy shrugged and smiled at his best friend. He hadn't yet had a chance to tell Chad the whole story. He raised his shoulders and shrugged. "I'm really sorry, man," Troy said. "No more secrets."

Chad grinned. "No more secrets," he agreed, and shook his friend's hand.

Then Troy whispered to Chad, "Looks like

you got your game back with Taylor." He nodded toward Taylor, who was sitting on the blanket next to Chad.

"Yeah," Chad replied. "We worked it out."

"Maybe you should get some kind of award, too," Troy joked.

Chad grinned over at Taylor. "I've got Taylor talking to me again. And that's definitely reward enough."

A few more Wildcats went on to tell stories, and Sharpay and Ryan even performed a musical number. They both held on to the stick as they harmonized a duet about a walk in the woods. Even Ashley got into the spirit of the evening and told a story about when she was five and went on a hot-air-balloon ride.

When everyone who wanted to speak had taken a turn, Ms. Darbus took the stick in her hands again. "Thank you all for sharing these insightful and entertaining stories. I think that you all captured the true essence of the talking stick. Bravo to all of you!"

"What about the awards?" Ashley called out.

"We're getting to that," Mr. Gold said. "But we still have one more challenge for the blue and green teams." He pointed over to a clearing to the right where there were two sets of poles with a thick rope tied across each one. "We're going to have a rope-burning contest," Mr. Gold explained.

"Hey, I did this at camp when I was younger!" Jason said enthusiastically.

"Yeah, me, too," Chad said. "It's awesome!"

Mr. Gold explained the rules. There would be six people chosen from each team to help build a fire. They'd all have to work together to create a flame tall enough to reach a rope that hung across two poles about six feet high. They would gather the items to be burned from the under-brush in the forest nearby and would use a sparker to start the fire.

Ranger Lou explained, "Though this is a fun activity, it is also beneficial forest management. By removing the loose underbrush, we improve the overall forest health and reduce the risk of forest fires."

"Nice," Chad said.

"Let's get to it!" Martha cheered.

The group quickly split into teams, and Kelsi and Martha picked the people who would represent them. Troy, Zeke, and Martha were part of the green fire team, and Chad, Jason, and Gabriella were part of the blue. Everyone was eager to get started.

When Mr. Gold shouted, "GO!" the teams raced to gather loose underbrush, fallen branches, dried leaves, sticks, and pine needles.

"Just grab all that you can!" Troy called to his green teammates as they ran toward the edge of the forest.

Gabriella did one sprint into the woods for material and then she got to work building the fire. As the other kids continued to return with material, she carefully placed the kindling, leaves, and pine needles at the bottom and stacked the wood in a pyramid, keeping enough space between each level so that the fire could breathe. All her camping trips with her mom had proven to be a good experience in not only tent-raising, but fire-building as well. As she applied the sparker, the leaves began to smoke and then her fire surged to life.

The green team was more concerned with gathering a large stockpile of firewood close by, and so they didn't start their fire until well after the blue team. Martha was sure that building a tall, steady structure would be the key to success.

Meanwhile, the rest of the green and blue teams were cheering from the sidelines. Everyone was screaming to build the fire faster and higher. The blue team's early start had allowed them to get within a few inches of their rope, which was starting to blacken and smoke. It looked like they had the competition in the bag.

"I can't watch!" Kelsi whispered to Ryan.

"I know," Ryan said. "And look, Martha has some tall flames." Just then, the green team's fire surged upward rapidly. "They've reached the rope!"

The green team was cheering loudly now. Sharpay and Ashley were jumping up and down. The fire was lapping at the rope. The rope was now red and spewing black smoke.

Not to be outdone, Chad raced back to the forest for one last armful of wood. Running back, he piled it on top of the blue team's fire, which made their fire leap even higher into the air. It was just the push they needed!

"We've got it!" Gabriella shouted. She sighed with relief as their rope finally stopped smoking and caught fire.

But just at that moment, the green's team rope split in two.

"The green team wins!" Mr. Gold declared.

As Martha's team cheered their victory, the blue team's rope gave way. Gabriella looked over at Kelsi. She felt terrible. She felt like she had let down her friend.

"You did your best," Kelsi said, seeing the look

on Gabriella's face. "I'm happy for the green team."

"Man, I thought that we had them!" Chad cried, kicking the dirt with his shoe.

But he didn't have too much time to pout. Mr. Gold clapped his hands together. "It's time to announce the winner of the scavenger hunt!" he called. "Everyone please take a seat and we'll begin."

The students moved back around the main bonfire to hear Mr. Gold's announcement.

Gabriella and Troy sat down next to Kelsi and Ryan. Gabriella could tell that Kelsi was nervous. She gave her friend a big smile of encouragement.

Mr. Gold began to walk around the circle. "I am so pleased with how this trip went. You all proved to be excellent scientists and showed me that you are observant and caring environmentalists. I want to thank Kelsi and Martha for their leadership and for taking special care to bring our blue and green teams to a very exciting and close finish."

"Who won?" someone called out.

"I'm getting to that!" Mr. Gold responded with a gentle smile. "After reviewing the two boxes, we have concluded that the winner of the scavenger hunt is . . ." He paused and looked around at the faces of his students. "The blue team!"

There was a loud roar from the crowd, and someone started chanting, "Blue rocks! Rock it to the top!"

"Stand up, Kelsi!" Gabriella urged, pushing her friend up to accept the award.

With a bright red face and a wide smile, Kelsi stood up and made her way over to her teacher. Mr. Gold shook her hand and beamed at her. "Kelsi, you and your team did a fantastic job. As a result, you all receive thirty points of extra credit."

Again, the blue team cheered. But the green team was not nearly as thrilled. Sharpay stomped her foot and scowled, while Ashley huffed. Martha folded her arms across her chest, but she couldn't help but smile. Kelsi looked so happy, and Martha had to be pleased for her friend. Kelsi would have been happy for Martha if the results were reversed.

Kelsi held up a hand, and her team quieted down. "I just want to thank everyone on my team for doing a fantastic job," Kelsi said to the crowd. She was trying not to think about how many pairs of eyes were on her at that moment. It was actually easier to address the crowd at night as she couldn't really see who she was talking to.

"And I want to thank the green team and Martha Cox for being such challenging opponents," she went on.

Martha stood up and waved. While she never liked to lose a tournament or a challenge, she was a good sport. "Thanks, Kelsi," she said.

"Well, if you would all let me finish," Mr. Gold said. "I have a few more announcements to make."

The crowd grew quiet. "The green team made many excellent observations and had several very good essays," Mr. Gold continued.

"Green machine!" someone cheered.

"Yes," Mr. Gold agreed. "A fine green machine! So after careful consideration, I am awarding the green team the same extra credit as the blue team."

There were several hoots and hollers from the crowd.

Sharpay traded high fives with Ryan. "I will so be driving that car soon!"

When Mr. Gold was finished, Ranger Jessica stood up and talked about the various ecosystems they had observed and how often nature versus nurture is a strong factor in environmental growth. "As they told you, if Gabriella and Troy had not called our attention to the young owl, he most likely would not have survived outside the nest."

Troy looked over and smiled at Gabriella. Her eyes were filling with happy tears.

"We'd like to award these two students with a special Ranger Award," Ranger Jessica said. "So please join me in cheering as they come up here to accept these certificates."

Together, Troy and Gabriella went over to Ranger Jessica. They were both very proud, and also a little embarrassed about all the praise.

"Way to go!" Taylor cheered.

"Good work!" Kelsi added.

But there were more awards to come. Next, Ms. Darbus stood up. When the chorus of crickets was all that could be heard, she began.

"We'd now like to award Taylor, Ryan, and Kelsi with a special certificate," Ms. Darbus said. "Their examination of a water sample led Ranger Lou to discover a problem in the water's algae balance."

Taylor, Ryan, and Kelsi stood up and walked over to their teachers.

"Good work," Ms. Darbus said, handing them each a certificate. She glanced down at the next paper in her hand. "And finally, I'd like to present Ms. Sharpay Evans with an award."

Sharpay straightened her sweater and patted

her head to make sure that every hair was in place. She smiled at the audience.

"With careful detail and thought, Sharpay's essay on bird mating was insightful and very informative," Ms. Darbus said, beaming. "Please come forward to get your award for best extra-credit essay."

With great flair, Sharpay walked up to receive her special award. Even though there was no stage, Sharpay still made it seem as though she were standing in a spotlight. She grinned at Ranger Mike, who had been her mentor for the essay. "The science of bird mating behavior is very interesting," Sharpay told the group. "I'd like to thank Ranger Mike for helping me and for showing me all the different species of birds that live here in the wild."

A few people applauded, and then Sharpay made her way back to her seat. Ashley didn't look so happy, but when Ranger Mike looked over their way, she smiled supportively at Sharpay and pretended to be excited for her award.

With that portion of the evening concluded, it was time for the trip's last event. The sky had grown dark and the inky night was cloudless.

Gabriella sighed. The night-sky lesson was going to be the perfect end to the perfect trip.

CHAPTER EIGHTEEN

"At the count of three," Ranger Lou said, "I want you all to switch off your flashlights. One, two, three!"

Lying on their sleeping bags, the students quickly turned off their lights. As soon as their eyes had adjusted to the dark, there was a loud gasp. They had moved away from the bonfire, and looking up they saw that the night sky was full of stars previously hidden. The stars twinkled brightly with no clouds or lights to obstruct the view. Even the Milky Way was visible.

Looking around at all his friends, Troy felt a sense of peace settle over him. Gabriella glanced at Troy and smiled. She, too, was feeling great and enjoying the night.

"Man, it's like being in a planetarium at a laser light show," Jason called out.

"An excellent one!" Chad added. "Cue the music."

"No music yet," Ranger Lou said. "At this show, we are here to study the stars. We need to enjoy being far from any cities where the light reflects, resulting in poor visibility. Out here, in this spot, we have the best chance for looking at and studying the night sky."

"And it's kind of romantic, too," Gabriella whispered in Troy's ear.

Troy smiled and looked up at the sky. "Yeah, I couldn't have planned a better date."

"You gotta love a class where you are told to lie down!" Chad added.

"Shhh," Taylor scolded. "I want to hear everything that Ranger Lou is saying." The smile on her face told Chad that she wasn't really angry, but Chad had learned his lesson. He didn't say another word.

Ranger Lou went on to point out a few clusters of stars in the sky. "Can anyone tell me what a constellation is?"

Taylor's hand shot up like a rocket. She, of course, knew the answer. "The term is used to denote a group of stars visibly related to each other in a particular configuration or pattern."

"That's correct," Ranger Lou said. "We can study the sky and recognize certain shapes and patterns. In the past, explorers used the constellations and particular stars—like the North Star—to help guide them before there were maps."

Zeke leaned over to Sharpay. He pointed up to the sky. "Those three stars are part of Pegasus, a constellation named after the mythological winged horse."

"Cool," Sharpay said, watching Zeke trace the horse's figure with his finger.

"Whoa!" Jason bolted up. "Did you see that shooting star?"

"I did!" Gabriella shouted. "It was over there." She pointed to the eastern part of the sky. "I think that it's good luck to see a shooting star."

"Like you need any luck," Ashley muttered. But even her barb didn't have much heart. It was hard to be angry in such a beautiful setting.

There were telescopes set up, and after the ranger's talk many people lined up to view the stars through the powerful lenses.

Gabriella preferred to watch the sky lying next to Troy, with her head on his shoulder. "This has been an unbelievable trip," she said. "I feel like we've been away from East High for longer than just a couple of days."

"I know!" Ryan piped up. "My back is killing me!"

"Oh, Ryan," Gabriella moaned, sitting up and giving him a playful tap.

"I need my lumbar-supportive mattress and Pilates class!" Ryan whined.

"And I would kill for my blow-dryer," Sharpay complained. "I am tired of wearing my hair up in a ponytail."

"You look great with your hair like that," Zeke told her.

She shrugged but didn't take her hair down. Then she wrapped her blanket around her shoulders and smiled.

Gabriella noticed that Sharpay wasn't sitting over by Ashley and the cheerleaders trying to get Ranger Mike's attention. Maybe Zeke *had* discovered the way to Sharpay's heart—a horse ride.

Ryan stretched his back out again. "But seriously, I am really glad that I came. Besides earning the extra credit and detecting a potential algae problem, I got to know Taylor better."

Taylor heard Ryan and gave him a smile. "Thanks," she said. "I had fun, too."

Looking up at the sky made Gabriella feel so

small. "We are just tiny specks in this huge universe," she said quietly.

"It's amazing, isn't it?" Kelsi said.

"I hope you all learned that environmental science is not just something that you study in a textbook," Ranger Lou said, moving over to their group. "You've got to live in the environment with your eyes and ears open."

"And take care of it," Gabriella said, smiling. She looked around at her classmates and thought about what they had all accomplished on the three-day trip. "We need to watch out for each other and all the living things in our world," she said.

"Good observation, Ms. Montez," Troy said.

"I couldn't have figured that out without you," she replied.

"Speaking of observations and learning, Ryan," Taylor said, "maybe you'd like to consider coming to some Scholastic Decathlon meetings."

Ryan shook his head. "I don't think that's really my show," he said. "But I had a blast being the crazy scientist with you." He stood up and put his hands straight out in front of him like Frankenstein, making Taylor laugh.

Just then, Ranger Jessica came over and gave Gabriella and Troy hugs. "Thanks again, you two," she said. "You know, we do have a Junior Ranger program here, if you'd be interested?"

Gabriella and Troy smiled at the ranger. It was a nice offer, and they were very flattered. But they politely turned her down. Getting out in the woods with their schedules seemed impossible. Still, they promised to keep in touch.

Hoooowwwwwwwwwwl. Hoooowwwwwwwwl. Hoooowwwwwl.

The sudden sound of coyotes in the distance quieted the group.

"I guess that our coyote friends are back," Kelsi said, looking a little nervous.

"At least it's not a bear," Jason said, looking over his shoulder. "No one sees a big hungry bear, do they?"

Gabriella smiled. "No, but I am kind of hungry."

"Is anyone else hungry?" Zeke asked, picking up on his cue. He looked over at Ranger Mike. "Any chance that we have any leftover s'more ingredients?"

"You bet!" Ranger Mike exclaimed, jumping up. "Come with me, Zeke."

The lessons over for the weekend, Max took out his guitar and began strumming a song. And there, under the bright stars, the Wildcats sang along.

CHAPTER NINETEEN

"**H**as anyone seen Zeke?" Jason said as he sat down on the picnic table bench across from Chad the next morning. "He slipped out of his sleeping bag really early, and now he's not here."

Chad took a bite of eggs before he answered. "Maybe he went for a run?"

"No way," Jason said. "He left his iPod, and Zeke doesn't run without that."

Troy and Gabriella walked up to the table. Gabriella was getting used to having every meal with Troy and their friends. She had to admit she was sad that there was a large bus waiting to take them all back to East High after breakfast.

"What's going on?" Troy asked. He noticed that his friends seemed worried.

"We're just wondering where Zeke is," Jason said.

Gabriella sat down, opened her milk carton, and poured it over her cereal. "You know, Sharpay left really early this morning, too." She turned her head and looked around. "And I don't see her here either."

"Hmm," Jason said with a smile. "What's up with that? Sharpay and Zeke together somewhere?" He waggled his eyebrows a few times. "What's happening out here in the wild?" He smirked and slapped Chad on the back.

Just then, Zeke and Sharpay appeared at their table. "You called my name?" Zeke said. He was grinning and holding a Wildcats baseball cap in his hands.

Before anyone could answer, Sharpay flipped

her hair and pulled on Zeke's arm. "I'm gonna go get some granola." She gave a fast smile to the crowd and then turned to lean closer to Zeke. "I'm glad that you came with me this morning. It was fun. See you later."

As she walked off, Zeke sat down at the table. No one said a word. Zeke looked at the blank faces of his friends. "What?" he asked innocently. "Why is everyone staring at me?"

Jason's eyes went wide, and he nodded his head toward where Sharpay was standing. "What was that all about?"

Zeke shrugged. "Oh, well," he said, blushing. "Sharpay asked me if I wanted to help out with the horses."

Troy gave Zeke a tap on his back. "Zeke, my boy," he said. "You are a changed man."

"So you actually went back and hung out with the horses?" Jason asked. He was still in shock that this was the same friend who wouldn't even walk near a horse twenty-four hours ago.

"They're not so bad," Zeke said, picking a piece of fruit off of Jason's plate. "It was fun. We fed Beau and the others and then groomed them a bit." He smiled at his friends as they sat silently watching him. "I'm going to go get some food. Those eggs look good." Getting up, he looked back at the table. "Try not to chat too much about me while I'm gone," he said with a laugh.

"You rock!" Chad said to Zeke. "You did a total one-eighty and that is awesome."

"Watch out, horses of the world!" Jason called out. "There's a new rider in town."

Everyone laughed. When it was quiet, Gabriella looked around at her friends. "This has been so great. I'm going to miss this place."

"Yeah," Troy agreed. "Me, too." He winked at Gabriella and gave her shoulder a squeeze.

"Oh, no," Ashley moaned as she walked by the table. "I don't know if I can take anymore."

Gabriella didn't pay any attention to Ashley. She wasn't about to let a nasty comment take away from their last meal at the campground. She focused her attention on Troy and sat happily eating her cereal.

Meanwhile, Kelsi, Ryan, and Taylor were meeting with Ranger Lou. The ranger had asked them to come to his table when they were finished eating their breakfast. "We have a project that you might be interested in," Ranger Lou said to the threesome. "I spoke to Mr. Gold, and he seemed to feel that you'd be perfect."

Taylor leaned forward. "What do you have in mind?" she asked.

"There is a lake a few miles from here where the rangers have been watching the water balance, and there is some concern that the levels are increasing toward dangerous," the ranger explained. "We were hoping that the three of you might like to sign on as part of a task force to try and uncover what is happening to the water. It would involve coming back throughout the year for day trips."

"Really?" Ryan exclaimed. He couldn't believe

that out of all the Wildcats, the ranger had chosen the three of them.

"That sounds like a great opportunity," Kelsi said, feeling proud of the way her team had performed over the weekend. She grinned at her friends. They could really make a difference by volunteering.

"We need people who are willing and knowledgeable to help us continue to test the water and keep a close eye on the levels," Ranger Lou went on. "What do you think? Would you like to join the team?"

Taylor, Kelsi, and Ryan started jumping up and down.

"From the looks on your faces," Ranger Lou said, "I'll take that as a yes."

"Yes!" they all said at the same time.

"What are you all excited about?" Ms. Darbus asked, coming over to the table.

"These three here have just agreed to help us out on a special project," Ranger Lou replied happily.

Ms. Darbus smiled. "I am not surprised. The students at East High are caring and studious. We're all very proud of them."

"And that is a tribute to their fine teachers," Ranger Lou said, tipping his hat.

Blushing, Ms. Darbus giggled. "Oh, well, thank you so very much. That is so kind of you."

Taylor nudged Kelsi and Ryan. "I think we should give them some space," she whispered with a silly grin.

The three of them slipped away from the table quickly as Ms. Darbus continued to blush and laugh.

"That's a match made in heaven, huh?" Kelsi said.

"Hmm," Ryan said, turning around to check out the couple. "They do seem to be hitting it off."

"Seems like everyone had a good time this weekend," Kelsi said. "But I need to go pack up my stuff."

"Me, too," Ryan said. "Man, I'm gonna sleep really well tonight!"

After breakfast was cleaned up and all the Wildcats had packed up their things, Mr. Gold had everyone gather one last time in a large circle. "I hope you all had a good weekend," he said to the group. "And I hope that you have come away with some new knowledge and an appreciation for our environment."

"And for my bed at home," Ryan whispered to Sharpay.

Sharpay smiled at her brother. "I can't wait to jump under that down comforter, and be around all my clothes again," she said. "And I am in desperate need of a mani/pedi. Look at my fingers and toes!" She scowled at her broken and chipped nails. "This has been a grueling experience."

"But fun, right?" Ryan said. "I bet you had more fun than you expected."

Laughing, Sharpay noticed that Ranger Mike had come over to the circle. For a moment she was tempted to get up and sit by him. But then she looked at Zeke and the feeling vanished. She was happy right where she was. "I always have a good time, Ryan," she said. "You should know that!"

Ryan rolled his eyes but he hid the smile when he noticed Sharpay didn't move.

"Please give a Wildcat thank you to our rangers," Mr. Gold said to the group. "They were wonderful hosts here at the campground, and I think that we all learned a lot from them."

Everyone cheered and hollered thanks as the rangers stood up and waved.

"Now, please gather your belongings and head to the bus," Mr. Gold instructed.

"Back to civilization!" Ashley cried, rushing over to the bus.

Gabriella let out a big sigh. She really didn't want to leave. Troy put his arm around her shoulder.

"Come on Ranger Gabriella," he said. "Let's go get some seats together."

Smiling, Gabriella was glad that at least she didn't have to say good-bye to Troy. She'd get to see him in school tomorrow. And that made her happy.

As the students climbed on the bus, the rangers stood in a line. After the various activities and bonding, all the Wildcats had their favorites and they wanted to make sure they said their good-byes.

"Do you want to hear some music?" Chad asked Taylor as they sat down together on the bus.

Taylor grinned at Chad. "Sure, I didn't get to hear that many songs on the ride up." She reached out and took a pair of earphones from Chad. "Thanks, Chad."

"Okay, everyone!" Mr. Gold shouted from the front of the bus. "I think we're ready to roll."

He motioned to the driver to close the doors and pull out of the campground.

"Wait! Mr. Gold!" Taylor called. "Where's Ms. Darbus?"

The bus driver stopped short. Mr. Gold got up and looked around. "Has anyone seen Ms. Darbus?" he asked.

There was a lot of whispering, and finally Troy called, "There she is!"

Everyone looked out the right side of the bus. Ms. Darbus was rushing toward the bus with her brown overnight bag in her hand. The doors opened and she leaped on.

"Oh, heavens!" She gasped with her hand on her chest. She took a moment to catch her breath. "I am so sorry. I completely lost track of time. Thank goodness I was able to catch you."

Mr. Gold gave Ms. Darbus a confused look, but he seemed very grateful that she was now onboard and that they didn't have to turn around to get her.

"I bet she wanted to say good-bye to Ranger Lou," Gabriella whispered to Troy.

"Ms. Darbus showing her wild side!" Troy joked.

Gabriella grinned. "So Ranger Troy, what songs do you know with the word 'star' in them?"

"A few," Troy said, picking up on Gabriella's

request to play the song game they had played on the way to the campground.

"Well, I've got plenty!" Gabriella teased. While she was sad to leave, she knew there was more fun ahead. There always was.

AVAILABLE NOW!

The must-have book for any fan of *High School Musical*

Includes lots of removable extras!

Experience the world of East High like never before with this complete behind-the-scenes guide to *High School Musical* and *High School Musical 2*!

Grab Your Gear And
Get Ready To Rock!
DON'T FIT IN.
STAND OUT.
CAMP
DISNEY
CAMP ROCK
• Never-Before-Seen Scene
• Go Behind The Scenes With Jonas Brothers And More!
Disney Channel
original movie
On Disney DVD And Disney Blu-ray August 19
DisneyChannelDVD.com
Distributed by Walt Disney Studios Home Entertainment, Burbank, CA 91521. ©Disney